kiss & Tell

Julia Blake

copyright ©Julia Blake and
Sele Books 2021
All rights reserved

Sele Books
www.selebooks.com

This is a work of fiction. All characters and events in this publication, other than those in the public domain, are either a product of the author's imagination or are used in a fictitious manner. Any resemblance to actual persons, living or dead, or actual events is purely coincidental.

No part of this publication may be reproduced, distributed, or transmitted in any form or by any means, without the written permission of the author, except in the case of brief quotations embodied in critical reviews and certain other non-commercial uses permitted by copyright law.

For permission requests contact the author.

www.juliablakeauthor.co.uk

ISBN: 9798731141406

Kiss & Tell is written in British English and has an estimated UK cinema rating of 12+ containing mild violence, occasional bad language and mild sexual references

Kiss & Tell is an Authors Alike accredited book

~Dedication~

To so many wonderful people.
To my Instagram Family, thank you.

To my wonderful daughter.
I am so proud of you.

~ *Acknowledgements* ~

Thank you must also go to my eagle-eyed beta reader, Caroline Noe. A talented author in her own right, you can find her at:

carolinenoe.org

Finally, a massive thank you to James and Becky Wright at Platform House Publishing for all their patient help with formatting and all their advice and creative input with the fabulous cover and interior graphics. Thanks, guys, you are amazing.

For all your publishing needs, contact Becky on:

www.platformhousepublishing.co.uk

~A Note for the Reader~

After the success of Lost & Found, Fixtures & Fittings, and Sugar & Spice I had so many readers contact me wanting to know more about the Blackwood family, begging for more stories.

Kiss & Tell follows straight on from Sugar & Spice and is Isabella Santorini's story. Although tough and more than capable of taking care of herself, Isabella finds herself faced with making the hard choice between what her head knows to be right, and what her heart wants to believe.

I have taken shocking liberties with just about every law enforcement agency and international law there is, all for the purposes of the story, so please forgive me.

As always, you can contact me on:
Facebook: Julia Blake Author
Instagram: @juliablakeauthor

And you can read all about my crazy life on my weekly blog "A Little Bit of Blake" on

https://juliablakeauthor.home.blog

You can also find out all about me and my books on my website:

www.juliablakeauthor.co.uk

~ *The Blackwood Family* ~

ONE
Legend of a Man

THREE
Very Different Wives

SIX
Individual Children

SEVEN
Extraordinary Tales

This is…

*THE
BLACKWOOD
FAMILY SAGA*

~A Family History ~

The Blackwoods are a wonderful, eccentric, rambling family. To quote Luke Blackwood – "they might be a hotchpotch of exes, steps and halves, but they're my family and I love them."

Originally founded by George Blackwood, a legendary fighter of a man, he and his first wife Celeste built a business empire between them and had two children, Monica and Marcus. But pressure soon split the perfect family cleanly down the middle with Celeste returning to her native New York and taking Monica with her, Marcus remaining in Britain to be raised by his father to take over the business one day.

George then fell immediately into another marriage with Marina, and for a while, things looked to be going his way, especially with the rapid arrival of their two children, Luke and Susannah. However, George was soon left heartbroken when this marriage also disintegrated, with Marina stating she would always love him but could no longer stand the pace of his life and of always coming second to his business. The pair remained firm friends, Marina even taking on the upbringing of George's eldest son, Marcus.

Alone and working too hard, the inevitable happened and George was hospitalised following a heart attack. Regaining consciousness after surgery, the first thing George saw were the laughing green eyes of his Irish nurse, Siobhan.

Two months later the pair were married, and despite the thirty years age difference between them, were blissfully happy for ten years, during which time Siobhan bore him two children, a son called Liam and a daughter called Kristina (Kit).

The whole family were devastated when George, by then in his late sixties, suffered another heart attack and died, leaving behind three women who had all loved him passionately in their own way, six children and one granddaughter, Megan, the child of his eldest daughter, Monica.

He also left behind a sizeable legacy to be split evenly between them, a multi-million business empire now ably run by his eldest son, Marcus, and a deep-seated work ethic tempered by bone-deep integrity and a sense of morality.

So that's the state of affairs in the Blackwood family at the beginning of this book. Luke, Marcus, and Susannah are now married and you can read their adventures in Lost & Found, Fixtures & Fittings, and Sugar & Spice – books one, two and three of the Blackwood family saga. Liam is a war photographer, and Kit is an up and coming opera singer.

All are happy and settled in his or her life, and each has no idea of the adventures they are about to embark on.

kiss & Tell

Book 4 of the
Blackwood Family Saga

Julia Blake

~Chapter One~
"I hate wearing wigs,"

The PA the agency had supplied to cover his own whilst she was off sick was easy on the eye – even if she did seem as dumb as a box of bricks. Tall, with long blonde hair and a body that would make a man weep.

As she collected his now empty coffee cup, his eyes wandered hungrily over those toned curves showcased nicely under the trim pencil skirt and form-hugging, sheer blouse.

"Will that be all, Signor Ricci," she murmured.

"Thank you, my dear," he oozed and beamed the dazzling smile that had cost a small fortune at her. She blinked, looking flustered. Good heavens, was she blushing? He didn't think young women did that anymore.

"The gentlemen for your midday meeting are waiting in the conference room," she informed him, and he hastily gathered his lustful thoughts to the matter in hand.

"Of course, thank you, umm…"

"Tiffany, Signor."

"Yes, Tiffany. Please could you arrange coffee for us all."

"Of course, do you need me to take notes?"

"No, just deliver the coffee and then leave us."

Tiffany nodded and left the room. Ricci sighed, watching her go. Perhaps not. It never paid to mess on your own doorstep, even if the girl was only a temp.

She had proved very satisfactory though, over the two days his own PA had been absent – and that reminded him – flowers. He would get Tiffany to arrange that.

Wondering at his reliable PA being sick for the first time he could remember, and hoping it wasn't contagious, he straightened his tie and strolled into the conference room, where granite-faced, and steely-eyed men awaited him.

They paused when the soft knock at the door heralded the arrival of the lovely Tiffany with coffee, and Ricci watched in amusement as the men straightened in their chairs, their eyes predatory as she placed the tray on the table and handed around coffee, asking each his preference for cream or sugar.

"Beautiful," one growled in Italian. "Magnificent breasts. Have you had her yet?"

Instinctively, Ricci glanced at the girl, but her face was impassive, and he remembered her denial of speaking any language but English.

"Don't be an animal, Ronaldo," he teased, and there were soft chuckles from the others.

Tiffany glanced up at them, clutching the edge of the large table as she looked from man to man, aware they were possibly laughing at her, but unsure why.

"Thank you, Tiffany," Ricci said. "That will be all for now."

"Yes, Signor," she said, and left the room, aware of the male eyes on her shapely rear end as it moved enticingly in her tight skirt.

"Now gentlemen," Ricci continued, dismissing the alluring Tiffany and her perfect curves from his mind. "Shall we get down to business?"

Signor Ricci would have been very surprised to see – if he *could* see through the solid wood of the conference room door – that the lovely Tiffany had abandoned her post at her desk and slipped silently into his office.

"Is it working?" she murmured.

"Loud and clear," the voice in her ear assured her. "We can hear everything that's being said, and the transmission is steady."

Quickly, Tiffany reached into her bra and pulled out a USB stick which she inserted into Ricci's computer. "You should be in," she said.

"Initial contact made," the voice in her ear confirmed. "Now breaking through firewalls. Honestly, the security on this is pathetic, a child could hack it."

A smile spread over Tiffany's face at this last comment. Only a child as brilliant as Seamus, possibly. Long seconds ticked by, and she glanced anxiously at the door.

The chances of Ricci leaving the meeting yet were slim, but not impossible, and she had no reason for being in here, on his computer.

"Come on," she muttered, impatiently tapping her fingers.

"Got it," the voice assured her. "Shadowing malware planted – from now on, we get to see everything he does on here."

"Extraction outside in five minutes," Tiffany ordered, plucking the USB from the computer, and ensuring all was exactly as Ricci left it.

Slipping from his office, the outer reception was still empty, and she took her jacket from the rack and her bag from under her desk.

Pausing outside the door to the conference room, she heard the rumble of male Italian voices raised in heated discussion inside.

Thinking of the bug discreetly palmed under the edge of the table when she had clutched at it in bemused embarrassment, she smirked.

"Pigs," she thought. "Magnificent breasts, huh." She glanced at them in satisfaction and hurried down the staircase, her heels rapping on the marble surface as she approached the front desk and pulling a face of anguish.

"Is anything wrong, Tiffany?" the kindly desk clerk asked, her matronly face showing concern at the downturned expression of the younger girl.

"I don't feel very well," Tiffany replied and clutched at her stomach in sudden alarm. "I don't feel very well, at all. I have to go home."

"Oh, my dear." The desk clerk managed to look sympathetic whilst keeping her distance. "No, you do look a bit pale, best you go home."

"Please can you inform, Signor Ricci. Tell him I'm sorry to leave early, but his normal PA should be back after the weekend, and I am up-to-date with my work."

"Of course, oh, go..." The clerk ordered as Tiffany clamped a hand to her mouth. "You go. I'll tell him when he's out of the meeting."

Nodding, Tiffany fled through the double doors and out onto the lunchtime streets of London. Once out of sight, her steps slowed, and she glanced around as a sleek limo with blacked-out windows pulled silently up to the kerb.

Sliding gracefully in, Tiffany slammed the door shut and thankfully yanked the blonde wig from her head and tossed it into the lap of the chisel-jawed woman sitting there.

"I hate wearing wigs," Isabella Santorini declared and ran her fingers through her short, cropped dark hair.

Kelly raised her eyebrows, and plucked the wig from her lap, dropping it into a bag at her feet and passing a neatly folded pile of clothes to Isabella who kicked off the elegant, low-heeled pumps she had been wearing and reached to undo the zip of the pencil skirt.

Wiggling out of it and the sheer nylons underneath, she pulled skinny fit jeans up over her hips and arched her spine to zip them up in the confines of the car.

"Mission successful?" Kelly asked, completely ignoring the backseat gymnastics as Isabella struggled out of the blouse and slipped into a sheer cotton tee-shirt in bronze khaki, dropping a chunky gold necklace over her head and thrusting her arms into a black blazer. Rolling up the sleeves, she fastened her Rolex onto her wrist and strapped ankle-breaking bondage sandals onto her feet.

Finally, Isabella wiped Tiffany's pink lipstick off and squinted into the mirror Kelly helpfully held up. Expertly smudging on eyeliner and a bright slash of scarlet lipstick, Isabella studied her reflection and decided she would do.

"Yes, completely successful," she finally answered. "Liaise with Seamus. I think I can guarantee the contents of Ricci's computer, plus what's being discussed in that meeting will prove beyond a shadow of a doubt that Ricci

Enterprises is a front for gunrunning to the Middle East."

"Who do you think our client is this time?" Kelly asked, and Isabella shrugged.

"Who cares – given the company's base in Milan it's likely to be the Italian's, but as the deals are being brokered in London, it could be the British. I don't negotiate the contracts; I only make sure they're carried out successfully."

Kelly nodded, then her poker face relaxed for a split second for a slight flush to touch those perfect high cheekbones and a considering gleam to twinkle in her eyes. "Is it true?" she asked.

"Is what true?" Busy threading gold hoop earrings into the reluctant holes in her ears, Isabella looked up at the other woman's words.

"That the big chief himself is visiting us?"

"Yep, next week, if all goes to plan."

"I've never met him," Kelly said. "But I've seen his pictures. He's very..."

"He is," agreed Isabella with a grin. "Very."

"Are you and he?"

"What?"

"Involved?"

"Lord, no. I'm so not his type, and he's *totally* not mine. No, we just have an excellent working relationship. He pays the bills and leaves me to get on with it. No interference, well, not much, and that's the way I like it. How do I look?"

"You look fine," Kelly assured her and handed her a handbag to match the shoes. "Your phone, wallet, and keys are all in there."

"Thanks." Isabella dropped the items of make-up she had used into the bag and glanced at her watch. "How are we doing for time?"

"We will be there in precisely three minutes. The others have already arrived and are perusing the menu and chatting whilst they wait for you."

She paused, a wistful note creeping into her usual professional tone. "They seem nice..."

"They are, they're family, so they are the best."

"You're lucky."

"I am," Isabella agreed, then fumbled for the door handle as the car slid to a halt. "I'll see you back at base – start translating the meeting, and I'll look at it when I get back."

"Sure thing, have fun."

Isabella nodded, strode from the car, and walked confidently around the corner to the restaurant where she'd agreed to meet the others. It was a beautiful early September day. A breeze whispered through her hair and Isabella's spirits lifted, a spring lightening her step.

"There she is!" Arianna exclaimed as she approached their table.

"Hi there, sorry I'm late." Isabella embraced her sister-in-law warmly, then turned to the others. "How is everyone?" she asked.

"Fine," Susannah assured her.

"Good holiday? You look great, nice tan."

"Can't think how I managed to get it," Susannah muttered. "Although we've been married almost five months, we've had hardly any time together, so this holiday we made up for it and barely left the hotel room."

The women laughed, and Isabella gently dropped a hand on the hugely rounded, nine months pregnant belly of Grace.

"How's my newest nephew doing?"

"Kicking his poor mother to death," Grace sighed, then grimaced when, as if to prove her right, Isabella's hand jumped at the sudden lurch under the skin.

"Oh, wow," Isabella looked down in wonder. "I felt that."

"Unfortunately, so do I," Grace complained. "All the time."

"Poor Marcus," the last member of their party laughed. "Does he have any idea what he's let himself in for?"

Isabella smiled at Kit Blackwood as she eased down into a chair and tucked her bag by her feet. Although she had met Kit before, she hadn't had a chance to spend much time with the young, up-and-coming opera singer.

"Hello, you," she said. "I didn't know you were back in England?"

"We're doing a gala charity event for the Prince's Trust, so I'm back for a few weeks."

"The Prince's Trust, hey?" Isabella teased. "Well, that definitely calls for a bottle of champagne, my treat, to celebrate."

"Oh, not fair," Grace sighed.

"Sip the bubbles," Isabella suggested and laughed at the face Grace pulled as the women settled down to the serious business of selecting their lunch choices.

Calling the waiter over and requesting a chilled bottle of champagne and five glasses, Isabella glanced around at her friends. These women she now considered her family, even though unconnected by blood. Tied as they were by bonds of marriage and friendship to form one loyal clan. She loved them all.

She would die for them. Would kill for them. And being Isabella Santorini, that was something she could do quite easily.

~Chapter Two~
"I came back for you,"

They lingered over coffee, each woman reluctant to be the first to leave the cosy group of like-minded friends who genuinely loved and admired each other.

Eventually, though, Arianna glanced at her watch and sighed.

"School run, I have to collect Lucia, and Luke has been alone with Josh all day, so we need to get home and relieve him as well."

"I'll come with you," Grace offered.

The two women departed amongst a round of hugs and promises to speak soon.

"Do you fancy coming shopping with me to help pick out a gown for the performance?" Kit asked her sister, and Susannah's eyes lit up.

"Definitely," she agreed.

They both looked at Isabella.

"It sounds fun," she said. "But I think I've played hooky long enough today. I need to get back to work."

"Must you?" Susannah asked, then quickly added. "Yes, I suppose you must, I know sometimes those IT assignments just can't wait."

Her eyes met Isabella's in a teasing manner, and Isabella's lips quirked into a smile. Susannah was fully aware that the IT job description was merely a front for the more *interesting* line of work Isabella was in. But she said nothing, merely hugged and kissed them goodbye, with promises to see them soon.

Walking slowly home through the late afternoon shoppers, Isabella found herself thinking about the career she had chosen for herself.

She loved it, of course, she did, could not imagine doing anything else, but sometimes it was awkward – all the lying she had to do, the fact she could be called away at a moment's notice, and of course there was the danger.

Isabella was no fool.

She never took unnecessary risks, and she was good at what she did – probably the best in the business – but still, things could always go wrong.

She knew agents who had gone out and not come back. It was one of the perils of the job.

Suddenly, Isabella froze, her disbelieving eyes scanning the sea of faces in the street ahead.

Could it be?

Had she seen?

Swiftly, she moved to where she had thought she had seen … him.

Turning the corner, she saw the back of the head of the person she had thought – could have sworn – was him…

He paused in front of an office block, his head turning briefly to scan the crowded pavement, almost as if he had sensed her scrutiny. She saw his face full-on.

It *was* him.

Without thinking, Isabella followed him into the building in time to see him vanish into an elevator.

Taking the stairs two at a time, confident in her heels, she reached the next floor to see the elevator glide by without stopping.

Two more floors he bypassed, but on the next, she reached the top of the stairs as the elevator doors were sliding closed and he was entering a suite of offices at the far end. Corlux, the sign on the door read, but Isabella swept through almost without seeing it.

A busy open-plan office, full of ringing phones and chattering voices. No one paid her any heed and Isabella strode confidently through the office to the door at the far end, the door he vanished into.

There was a desk positioned outside, with the usual immaculate PA seated at it. Busy on the phone, the woman glanced up as Isabella hovered, and smiled at her.

Mouthing *just a minute*, she indicated the sofa to the left. Clearly wanting Isabella to take a seat and wait until she was done.

But Isabella couldn't wait.

Ignoring the PA's gasp of outraged surprise, she pushed the door open and entered a large, sunny office where he was sitting at a desk at the far end, his mouth opening in an *oh* of surprise, the phone held to his ear shaking in a suddenly unsteady hand as he stared at her.

"Hello, Nick," she said and tried to smile.

Behind her, the aggrieved PA hustled in, almost barging into Isabella in her haste to reassure Nick that this intrusion had not been her fault.

"I'm so sorry, Mr Eastman," the woman began. "She just walked in before I could stop her. Shall I call security?"

"No, Karen, that's fine," he assured her. "This is an old ... friend. It's fine. Please hold all my calls for a while."

"Yes, Mr Eastman."

Karen cast Isabella a dubious look, but left the office without another word, softly closing the door behind her.

Nick stared at Isabella until a voice squawking down the phone jerked him back into the moment.

"I'm afraid I'm going to have to call you back," he muttered into the phone. "I'm sorry, something's come up, yes, I will, soon, thank you, bye."

He hung up, then rose to his feet and moved from behind the desk to cross the room in two strides.

"Isabella?" he breathed. "Is it really you?"

He'd changed, she thought, unable to speak as her eyes roved over his face, seeing the lanky boy she once loved buried beneath the handsomely rugged man he became.

"Nick," she whispered.

His expression changed.

"I never thought I'd see you again," he murmured. "When you didn't meet me that night. I waited for you, but your brother came. He said you'd changed your mind and then he gave me back the locket I'd given you and your letter. Oh, Isabella, that letter...."

"I know."

Briefly she closed her eyes against the memory.

"He made me write it," she said. "He … hurt me until I did."

Nick's face darkened with anger at a deed done so many years before, but fresh with the sting of new discovery.

"I came back for you," he said. "At the end of my trip, before I returned to the States, I came back. I hammered on the door of your house but there was no one there. Then the gardener told me the house was locked up, that it was for sale and the family had gone away."

"I didn't know," Isabella replied. "I thought you probably hated me so much you would never want to see me again."

"Hate you? Oh, Isabella," he sighed, his face relaxing into fond memory.

"I could never hate you, no matter what I thought you'd done."

One hand rose to cup her face and in a heartbeat, everything changed.

It was still there.

The need.

The lust.

The absolute want.

The love.

It hadn't died, hadn't gone away.

It had just been buried under years of hurt and perceived rejection.

Isabella heard a sob erupt from her throat and hated herself for her weakness but couldn't help it.

It was him.

It had always been him.

She loved him still.

Probably always would.

The large hand slid to the back of her neck, and he was pulling her towards him.

She did nothing to stop him, instead, angled upwards to meet him. Even in her killer heels, he was still taller than her.

He kissed her.

They kissed each other, and time did a backflip to that never forgotten, magical summer when she was seventeen and thought the world was hers for the taking.

Those few months during which she met an American boy and lost her heart to him in a love affair that stunned them both with its strength and its passion.

When innocence was willingly surrendered, and promises made in the balmy Italian summer nights.

Then doubts and questions crowded in, and she raised a hand to push lightly on his chest.

"Nick," she murmured against his mouth. "Stop, please. There are things we need to talk about."

"I know."

He rested his forehead against hers and sighed.

"But first, I want to hold you. I missed you so much, Isabella. There has never been anyone for me like you."

"But there has been someone?" she ventured, and he shrugged.

"I tried – my college sweetheart I was dating before I left on my gap year. When I returned, she came to visit and I told her all about you, hell, I couldn't stop talking about you. She listened. She was the one who told me to look for you, so I did, all the next year, but I couldn't find you,

Isabella. It was like you'd vanished off the face of the earth."

"Yes," Isabella agreed quietly.

She'd been recruited by Sebastian by then, her identity hidden so only the very determined could find her address.

"And then, gradually, she became more than a friend. Looking back, I know she was just a shoulder that I'd gotten used to crying on. I should never have married her; it wasn't fair. But she said she understood, was happy with the pieces of my heart I could give her. Three months into the marriage, we both realised that was a lie. She's remarried now, with two kids. Her husband is a great guy, and he makes her very happy. I'm pleased for them."

Isabella nodded, unable to speak as his arms slipped around her and he hugged her into his chest so tightly she fancied she could feel his heart beating frantically against her.

"And you?" he asked. "Are you with someone?"

"No."

She shook her head against his shoulder.

"There's not been anyone since … I've been busy, and my life was complicated, and … no, there's no one."

"Isabella …"

He kissed her again and she wanted it so badly, wanted him so badly, that she did nothing to stop him, couldn't have done, even if she wanted to.

"We do need to talk," she finally said, and he nodded, his eyes never leaving her face.

"I'm in London for another month or so," he said. "I'm staying at the Hilton. Have dinner with me tonight."

"Nick, I'm not sure..."

"Have dinner with me, Isabella, please..."

Unable to refuse him, and unable to think of a single reason why she should deny herself this, Isabella agreed.

~Chapter Three~
"Do you want dessert?"

The Hilton dining room was understated and classy. Isabella was pleased she'd dressed accordingly.

Trying to relax, she leant on the table and studied Nick intently, unabashed as he raised his eyebrow at her scrutiny.

"See anything you like?" he drawled, and she smiled a slow curve of approval.

"I was looking at the changes. It's still you in there, but you've changed. You're a man now. I was looking for traces of the boy I knew."

"Oh, he's here," Nick assured her. "But I hit the gym hard when I got back. I also took up martial arts. I was determined not to be that skinny runt other guys kicked sand at anymore."

"Oh, you were never that," Isabella reassured him, then startled when one large, warm hand crept over the table to encase hers.

"You've changed too, Isabella. You were always pretty, but now, you're so beautiful, stunning. I like the short hair. And it looks like I'm not the only one who hit the gym."

"I like to keep in shape." Isabella shrugged, wondering what he would think if he knew of the months, and years, of training she had undergone to become what she was now.

He looked at her, his thumb rubbing gently at her skin, and Isabella's heart skipped a beat. Dry mouthed with sudden arousal, she stared into his eyes – those beautiful hazel eyes that she remembered so well.

Then the waiter was there, and they let go, grasping at menus and excuses to pull away from the intensity of the moment.

"So," Nick began when choices had been made and wine poured. "What line of work are you in?"

"IT," she told him, sipping with approval at the excellent Chenin Blanc. "And you?"

"I'm in the Boston branch of Corlux, but I'm over here for a few months learning the British side of the business."

"And Corlux is?"

"Oh, right, import and exports. Very boring."

"Not what you planned?"

"No, not what I planned."

"Do you still write?"

"A little, sometimes ... no, not really. There never seems time."

They paused as their appetisers were placed before them, each doing the obligatory appraisal of the other's plate before sampling their own.

"This is good," Isabella said, tasting the delicate flavour of the gravlax and the salad garnish with raspberry dressing.

"How's yours?"

"It's fine," he reassured, around a mouthful of Thai crab cake.

The meal progressed, and the talk eased into memory and nostalgic chat of those long-ago days.

Neither of them named what was lying on the table between them. That sharp pull, that made

Isabella want to fling convention aside and yank him across the place settings by that handwoven silk tie and plunder his perfect mouth again.

Instead, she shifted uneasily in her chair, her stomach roiling in anticipation. His eyes met hers in a warm sharing of acknowledgement and she knew he felt it too.

That absolute certainty of how this evening was going to end.

"Do you want dessert?" he asked when their main course had been cleared away.

"Not down here," she replied, and his eyes went opaque with desire.

There were others in the elevator on the way up to his room, so she stood demurely beside him, every fibre of her being thrumming with nervous anticipation.

She eased her little finger over until it was touching his hand. His finger linked with hers in return and that tiny connection sparked through her entire body.

With a clutch of amusement, Isabella felt herself go weak at the knees like some eighteenth-century bonneted heroine.

He looked at her.

She felt it burn even though she remained staring resolutely straight ahead.

The elevator reached his floor and they walked to his room. Fumbling with the key card, he let them in and then they were alone, in the darkness, and it was like when they were young but achingly better and seasoned with maturity and experience.

A thin dawn was breaking through the undrawn curtains when Isabella carefully arose and pulled on her clothes from the night before. Slipping on her shoes, she paused to look down at him.

Still sleeping, he was laying on his back with one arm thrown to the side of the bed she had lain on as if pleading with her to stay.

For a moment, she hesitated.

Some part of her longed to be there when he awoke, to roll into his arms and explore him all over again. Afterwards, to lie still and quiet, talking and maybe ordering breakfast to eat in bed together.

But Isabella needed to be alone, to assess and think about what this meant and how she felt about this reconnection with the only man she had ever loved.

In all her dreams about meeting up with Nick again, she had always imagined it would be as it was before.

Never had she thought how much better it would be, now that they were both adults with the confidence to know what they liked and ask for it.

She knew he would be disappointed she'd left, would probably not understand this dawn flit from his bed.

To soften the blow, because she did want to see him again – to see where this could lead – she left a note on the bedside cabinet.

Nick – last night was amazing. Sorry, I had to go but work and life, you know how it is. My number is below, call me. Please. Isabella.

She was happy with the note – it conveyed the right amount of reserve and enthusiasm.

It also put the ball squarely in his court. If he wanted to call her, he would. If he didn't, then ... well, that would be that.

An hour later, Isabella let herself into the peaceful stillness of her home. It took a while to find a taxi at such an early hour and she walked a great deal of the distance before hailing one.

The driver raised a brow at this woman doing the walk of shame but was thankfully of the non-chatty variety and merely took her home, grunting his thanks at the tip she gave him.

Now, Isabella wanted a shower, coffee, and breakfast to face another day at work, although knew she would hug the memories of the night to her heart, hoping Nick would call, expecting he probably would, but still, hoping...

Isabella closed the front door, then froze in the hallway, one hand still on the latch. Someone was in her home.

She could sense it.

Could tell by the partially ajar door to the lounge that she knew she closed firmly the evening before.

Suddenly alert, she silently oozed along the hallway and gently pushed on the door. A subtle waft of expensive cologne greeted her, and she relaxed, knowing who it was. She should probably have been expecting him.

Sighing, she pushed the door open to reveal the tall, dark-haired man sitting in the armchair. He quirked a smile as she entered – the cheeky bastard had helped himself to a glass of her expensive Scotch. At seven in the morning?

A reluctant admiration briefly flared, before she paused, hands on her hips, and surveyed him with annoyance at his intrusion.

"Sebastian?"

"Ah, Isabella, there you are. I was beginning to wonder if you were ever coming home from your ... ahem ... dinner date?"

"My dinner dates are absolutely none of your business, Sebastian. What are you doing sitting in my lounge, drinking my Scotch, this hour in the morning anyway? We weren't expecting you until next week."

"Yes, something has come up. A contract for an important client that needs to be handled sooner rather than later."

"And it couldn't wait until office hours?"

"Isabella, Isabella," he shook his head in amusement. "There is no such thing as office hours for us. And I did try your mobile last night and was a little concerned it went straight to voicemail each time."

Yes, she'd deliberately switched her phone off, an almost unheard-of occurrence. Wanting uninterrupted time for her reunion with Nick, to assess how she felt about him, about them ... and then she went to his room and...

"I am entitled to some private life, Sebastian."

"Of course," he agreed blandly, then his face relaxed into a smile, and he arose to his whole six feet plus of Italian male gorgeousness and moved to embrace her in a familial hug.

"How have you been?" he rumbled into her hair in a friendly enquiry. "I've missed you. It has been too long since you visited us. Mama is always asking after you."

Isabella relaxed into his hug, comfortable with him after a lifetime of intimacy. She then pulled away to flash her cousin a smile.

"Send her my love."

"I will," he promised. "But you should come and give it to her yourself. She misses you, Isabella. After the death of your parents, and then my father soon after. And of course, there was that unpleasantness with Roberto."

Isabella looked into the kindly concerned eyes of Sebastian Santorini – the only blood relation remaining to her, except for her niece, Lucia.

Memories stirred as she recalled the cousin, she had hero-worshipped since childhood, coming to see her soon after her brother had defrauded the bank where he worked of millions of pounds and absconded.

Lonely and adrift, she'd floated from job to job since leaving school. Missing Nick with an intensity that wouldn't heal, caring passionately for her sister-in-law Arianna and her baby niece, she'd been delighted when Sebastian called her.

He was in London, he said, could they meet? He had a proposition for her. She eagerly agreed, not realising that one meeting would change her life forever.

He had spoken to her seriously – after first making her swear to keep their conversation secret. That, should she repeat any of it, to anyone, she could be endangering not only his life but others as well.

Bemused, she promised. And then he told her. Her flamboyant, extroverted, playboy billionaire cousin had an alter ego.

He lived a whole other existence that was known only by a very select few. He ran a sort of business, he told her.

What sort of business? She asked in confusion, listening in disbelief as he explained that he headed an intelligence organisation of sorts.

Above the law, above any government, it had been founded jointly by many wealthy men from many nations to deal with certain *matters* that could arise to threaten the welfare of a country and its people.

Sometimes, government and law enforcement agencies had their hands tied by laws and diplomacy and protocols. Sometimes, it was *useful* to be able to call upon the discreet services of an organisation that was answerable to nobody but themselves.

Don't underestimate the appeal of plausible deniability to a government, he told her.

Unable to believe what she was hearing; Isabella truly thought he was joking until he took her to one of their bases of operation and she saw for herself the deadly serious nature of what he was saying – of what he was offering her.

A job, a career, a chance to do good and fight back against the evil in the world, a chance to be trained how to protect herself and those she loved in any given situation.

~Chapter Four~
"Fate brought us back together."

Isabella had accepted the job on the spot, and now almost a decade later, she had never had a cause to regret her spontaneous decision.

"But you still haven't told me why you're here, Sebastian," she continued. "I don't for one minute believe it's out of concern for my morals, so what is it?"

"There is a man our friends in the DEA are very interested in. A known drug lord, he goes by the name of The Preacher. He operates out of Afghanistan and is almost untouchable. He never moves without an army surrounding him. Up until now, he has contented himself with drug running in the Middle East with some markets in Asia. But now..."

"Now?"

"Drugs with his signature have been turning up on the streets of big cities in the US, and of course the Drug Enforcement Agency are keen to find out how they are coming into the country and put a stop to it."

"What do they want us to do?"

"There was a meeting, in Boston, a couple of months ago. They had an agent in on the ground who took some photos and managed to get them out before his cover was blown."

"What happened to the agent?" Isabella asked, even though she knew.

"He was found with a bullet through his head two days later. But the photos he sent, the men they managed to identify on it – that's where it gets interesting. They were mostly known to the DEA, men who have long been suspected to have connections to The Preacher, but…"

"But?"

"There was one face that was new to them, a man who'd never appeared before in any intel on The Preacher. Him, they are very interested in."

"So, are we going to America to find this guy?"

"No need, he's come to London, and naturally the British government are concerned that means The Preacher is planning to open up shop here, and this man is his facilitator."

"Do we have a name?"

"Yes, and I have a copy of the photo. It might be of some interest to you." He passed her an envelope, which Isabella took, puzzled by the sadness she saw lingering in Sebastian's eyes.

Sliding the photo from the envelope, she tipped it towards the early morning light now streaming in through the window and studied the group of men it portrayed, hunched in a group, furtively talking, in what looked like an old warehouse. It was clear from the body language and the number of weapons on display, that something illegal was going down.

Frowning, Isabella peered closely at each man's face and then she found him, and her heart stopped in denial.

"I am sorry, Bella," Sebastian murmured as she handed him back the photo. "We suspect that the company Corlux is a cover for the illegal import of drugs, and we're going to need to exploit your relationship with Nick Eastman to help us catch his employer, The Preacher."

Isabella thought to deny it, for a second, then realised the futility of it. There was a tracking device planted in her phone that would give away her location even if the phone were switched off.

As for Nick – they were watching him, of course, they were – would have been since the moment he arrived in the country.

Dispassionate eyes would have seen her join him for dinner at the Hilton, would probably even have known about her impromptu visit to his office. It would have been reported back.

Looking at Sebastian, Isabella knew precisely why he was in London a week earlier than scheduled. It was because of her.

Because she had been compromised.

"I'm sorry, Bella," he said again, as her silence stretched into awkwardness between them. "When I realised, he was the man you had a relationship with all those years ago, I intended to send you out of the country on a mission – get you away from the situation. You meeting him yesterday pre-empted my plans. Tell me, it *was* a coincidence, wasn't it?"

"Yes." At last, she found her voice. "A complete coincidence. I saw him on the street and followed him back to Corlux. It was just a coincidence."

"They happen." Sebastian shrugged away the vagaries of fate. "But now that contact has been made, we need to use it."

"Use me, you mean." There was no disguising the bitterness in her tone, and the sympathy in her cousin's eyes deepened.

"Bella..."

"Don't," she snapped and turned from him so he could not see the devastation in her eyes. She took a deep breath, struggling to gain control.

"What do you want me to do?"

"Get close to him, really close, learn as much as you can about him. We want to know why he is here, how far up the food chain he is, and most importantly, can he lead us to The Preacher? How were things left between you this morning?"

"I left him a note with my number," she mumbled. "I asked him to call me."

"Good," replied Sebastian in satisfaction. "When he calls, arrange another meeting."

"He might not call…"

"He will. This is a man who has been in love with the memory of you for over a decade. One night won't be enough for him, he'll want more."

"He might decide it's too dangerous to take it any further with me. After all, *if* he is what you say he is, then he would be foolish to risk it."

"Oh, he'll call."

"How can you be so confident?"

"I am confident in you," Sebastian said and placed a large warm hand on her cheek. "He will call – he won't be able to help himself."

Sebastian was right. An hour later, as Isabella nursed her second cup of coffee and wondering if she should force some breakfast into her reluctant body, her mobile rang, and it was him.

"Hi," she murmured, furious that her treacherous heart gave a leap of joy at hearing his voice; that even though she knew what he was suspected of doing, she still wanted him.

"Isabella," he said her name, then said it again. "Isabella … I missed you this morning –

you were gone when I woke up – I thought, that is, I'd hoped you'd still be there. That we could spend the day together."

"I have work," she replied.

"On a Saturday?"

"Sometimes, yes, I'm sorry … I wanted to stay, but I needed to go, to have time, to think…"

"I understand," and she heard from his voice that he did. "Can I see you again?"

Isabella hesitated. She knew what Sebastian wanted, what whichever government was footing the bill this time wanted, and she knew what her heart wanted. But her head was telling her to refuse, to protect herself from being hurt. Because she *was* going to get hurt. Isabella was no fool, she knew that agents got wounded in the field all the time; knew if she said yes, then her heart stood the risk of being seriously damaged.

"Isabella?"

"I'm not sure, is it wise? Last night was unbelievable, and I don't regret it for a moment. But is it sensible to take it any further?"

"Probably not," he agreed with an ironic bark of laughter. "But I'm prepared to risk it if you are. I must see you again, Isabella. Please, I must."

"Nick…"

"Tonight, I want to see you tonight. Say yes, Isabella, please, say yes."

"Yes," she said and sealed her fate.

He came to her house – Isabella couldn't have explained why, but she wanted it that way – wanted to be in control of the environment. And maybe it was because she knew her house wasn't bugged, that whatever occurred between her and Nick, there wouldn't be voyeuristic ears listening.

He arrived exactly at seven, bearing gifts of a large bouquet, chilled champagne, and hand-dipped chocolate truffles. The flowers slipped as he rang the bell, and she opened the door to find the bouquet being thrust at her as he desperately tried to stop their fall.

She laughed.

He laughed.

It got them through the awkwardness of that first moment. Of seeing each other again, after what happened in his hotel room.

He was dressed more casually this time, well cut, expensive-looking black jeans and a white linen shirt with its sleeves rolled up to combat the lingering heat of an Indian summer.

He looked good, and when he bent to press a kiss on her cheek – he smelt good too. For a moment, Isabella closed her eyes and allowed herself to pretend.

Then she pulled back and divested him of his armful of gifts, and time was filled as she led him to the kitchen to find a vase for the bouquet, gesturing towards the cupboard where she kept her champagne flutes when he enquired.

He opened the champagne, and they drank, Isabella returning his warm smile when he touched his glass to hers.

"You have a lovely home," he said, looking around the large, open-plan kitchen admiringly.

"Thank you, I like it," she replied, putting down her glass to slide the garlic bread into the oven to crisp.

"I've made Italian – I hope that's all right."

"Very," he replied. "That's another thing I missed about Italy, the food."

"Well, I'm not the greatest of cooks," she admitted. "But I do make a mean carbonara, and there's a tiramisu for after."

"Sounds great."

Silence fell between them, and they both reached for their glasses as something to do to fill the void.

"Why did you really leave this morning?"

Isabella sighed, meeting his gaze with a direct one of her own. "I needed time to think, to sort through in my head what had happened. To try and see how I felt about it. How I felt about you. About us…"

"I understand. And have you reached any conclusions?"

"I don't know. What we had back then, Nick, was so special, so wonderful … I never forgot you, never stopped wondering how it would have gone if Roberto hadn't caught me that night."

"We would still be together."

"But how can you be so sure, so confident," she cried out, in an agony of confusion.

Hold on, her head demanded. Slow down. You know what they suspect this man is, what they believe him capable of. I don't care, her heart protested. I need to know. I must know.

"I'm sure because I know how I felt about you back then, Isabella. I'm confident because I know how I still feel about you now."

"You've only just met me again … one night doesn't prove anything."

"To me it does."

He put down his glass and took hers, placing it on the counter behind them as he moved to wrap his arms around her.

"I know," he murmured, his stubble tickling her chin as he whispered kisses along her jawline and up to her ear.

"I know because I love you, Isabella. I always have and I always will. And I know after last night, that you still love me too. It doesn't matter how sensible or not it may be, fate brought us back together after so many years – and that cannot be a coincidence."

He pulled back and let her breathe, his eyes warm with an understanding of the impact of his words.

"I have something for you," he said, and Isabella raised her brows and pursed her lips.

"No, not that," he replied, having the grace to flush at her implication.

She raised her brows even further.

"Well, maybe that," he admitted sheepishly. "But also ... this."

He reached into his jeans pocket and drew something out which he placed gently into her palm and closed her hand around it.

~Chapter Five~
"I don't have to like doing it."

Speechless, Isabella gazed at him. Not needing to look, knowing from the feel of it precisely what he had given her, she felt her mouth dry with emotion.

"The chain was broken," he murmured, and she nodded.

"That's from when Roberto ripped it from my neck. I refused to give it to him, so he took it by force. I don't know how he knew it was a gift from you, but somehow, he did. He understood how precious it was to me, and what it would mean if it appeared as if I'd given it back to you."

At last, Isabella opened her hand and looked down at the delicate Victorian locket she held.

With fingers that shook, she fumbled at the clasp and the lid opened to reveal the tiny face of the watch on one side and the miniature photo of the girl she had once been on the other.

Her dark hair – long as it had been then – rippled over one shoulder as the young Isabella stared confidently out at a world, she was convinced was hers for the taking, at the boy, she had loved to distraction and trusted implicitly.

She remembered the day they found it in a small antique shop located on a side street off the harbour.

Musty with the dust of ages, the shop had been stuffed with keepsakes and knickknacks from a bygone era and they poked about its shadowy interior until suddenly, she heard him exclaim as he bent over a locked glass cabinet by the counter.

"Isabella, look," Nick muttered.

She crossed to stand beside him, following the direction of his pointing finger to the locket, open to show the perfection of the watch and the space opposite for a single photograph.

He looked at her and had known how much she wanted it, so bought it for her – despite her protests at him wasting so much of his hard-earned money on something so frivolous.

Later, in his room, he sorted through the dozens of photos he had taken of her and picked out this one as his favourite. Carefully he cut it down to fit and placed it in the locket.

"It should be a picture of you," she'd said.

But both had known they dare not risk it. That if it had been found by her parents, or by her brother, then their secret would be discovered.

"You kept it," she finally whispered, stunned beyond words that he had.

"I've carried it with me every day since then," he told her, his hand tracing over the watch in her palm and then up and onto her wrist.

"It was a reminder of you, of how much I loved you then. When I met you again, I knew it was time I returned it to you. Then, it was a gift from me to you, to show you how much I loved you. Now, it's a gift in the hope that you can love me again the way you once did."

Isabella shook at his words and then his mouth was on hers and all sense and all logic fled from her startled mind, and she was kissing him back, desperately wanting this man to love her again, and unable to resist the demands of her treacherous and foolhardy heart.

They ate dinner late. Sitting at the small table in her garden, they watched a perfect sunset as they lingered over their meal.

Both still barefoot, their clothes loosely pulled back on, their eyes and hands constantly met in an agony of passion.

It had been even better than the night before if that was possible. New familiarity made them confident with how to give, with what made each other happy, and now Isabella stretched in her chair as limber as a satisfied cat.

Hungry, Nick demolished his meal, finally pushing away his plate with a sigh of satisfaction.

"That was delicious," he exclaimed. "I can't remember the last time I had a good, home-cooked meal."

Isabella smiled but remained silent. Inside she was a torture of indecision.

She must question him, she knew that.

Find some way to extract the information that they needed.

"So," she began. "How long have you worked for this Corlux company?"

"Not long," he answered. "About six months in the States, then a month here. I'm still learning the ropes. I was headhunted from a different organisation, so I have a lot to learn."

"What sort of things does it import and export?" she asked, languidly refilling his glass.

"Oh, this and that, nothing very exciting."

He evaded her question with a laugh.

"But what about you? IT hey? What exactly do you do?"

"Oh, this and that," she replied and raised her brows at him.

"Perhaps I should get your company to come and look at our in-office system," he said. "It's a total mess, glitchy as hell, and slower than my Great Aunt Betsy."

"If you like," she offered casually, unable to believe the opportunity he was handing her on a plate.

"I'll talk to my supervisor about it on Monday. I'm sure they will be only too happy to give you a quote."

"Cool, but I'd want you to do the work, Isabella. I trust you. I remember what a perfectionist you were, even back then. I'm sure whatever job you do, you see it through to the bitter end."

"Well, if something is worth doing," she began.

"It's worth doing well," he finished, and they smiled at one another.

"Tell me," he asked, his voice a little husky. "Do I need to be booking a taxi back to my hotel? Or do you have a toothbrush I can borrow?"

Isabella hesitated.

Her head knew she should send him on his way. She'd made a start.

An opportunity to inspect the computer systems at Corlux and possibly extract all the information they required directly from them, would have Sebastian doing a little happy dance when she told him.

Her heart didn't want him to leave.

No, it wanted this man to stay. It wanted to take him by the hand and lead him to her bed and wrap herself around him.

She wanted to pretend – if only for one night – that they were normal people rekindling the flames from a long-ago holiday romance and seeing how fiercely they still burnt.

"Do you want dessert?" she asked.

"Not down here," he replied, and their eyes met in an agony of need and anticipation.

He stayed the night, and for most of Sunday. Every time she murmured a protest about needing to get up, he would pull her back down to him.

They had so much lost time to make up for, he told her, and so she let him stay.

But finally, he left, with kisses and promises to see each other soon, and then he was in a taxi and driving away, but not to his hotel as she thought.

Instead, he sent the taxi on a torturous route through London backstreets, before ordering it to drop him off.

After that, he led whoever was following him – because he knew someone must be even though they were so good he hadn't spotted them – on a merry dance through the subways, and alleyways of the big city.

At last, satisfied he had lost them, he stood in a darkened room where someone sat in the shadows.

"Well?" croaked the voice.

"She fell for it," Nick replied quietly, guilt almost strangling the words in his throat. "She's going to speak to her supervisor tomorrow and arrange a quote and an appointment."

"Did she suspect?"

"No, why should she? As far as she is concerned, it was a pure coincidence that she saw me on the street that day. I'm just a man she had a holiday romance with ten years ago trying to relive the glory days and reignite a dead love."

"Good," the voice paused. "And make sure that's how it stays for you. We don't want any ... *complications.*"

"There won't be," Nick assured the shadowy presence. "But are you sure she's what you think she is?"

"Having second thoughts, are you?"

"No, of course not. I know what must be done. I know what I need to do. It's just..."

"Just what?"

"I don't have to like doing it."

Corlux telephoned on Monday. Re-routed through the supposed receptionist of Henley IT Consultants to the phone in Sebastian's office, Isabella listened as he expertly pretended to be the contracts manager.

Of course, they would be only too happy to visit and assess the out-dated systems at Corlux. And of course, it could be Miss Santorini who came.

She watched Sebastian's face, thinking what an accomplished liar he was, as she was, as they all were within the organisation.

When one slip of the tongue or too slow an answer could get you killed, you learnt fast to think on your feet and always have a convincing reply at the ready.

But was it any way to live?

The question nagged at Isabella's mind and angrily she pushed it away.

"It's all set," Sebastian informed her after he replaced the phone. "Wednesday at 10am. You're to go in with your box of tricks and see what you can do. If you get the chance to plant shadowing malware, that would be excellent. But you might not be left alone this first appointment, so, do the best you can."

"I know what to do" she replied, her voice sandpaper dry at the thought of lying to Nick, of using her expertise to expose him.

Sebastian gave her a long, considering look, then he abruptly nodded and turned his attention to the heap of paperwork on his desk.

"There's absolutely no shadow of a doubt he's guilty, is there?" Isabella demanded. "I mean, how sure is the DEA that Nick Eastman is in league with The Preacher. The Nick I knew was as straight as a die, he'd never be involved in anything like this."

"People change, Isabella. The Nick you knew was a young, idealistic boy of 19. The Nick you are now dealing with is a man of 30. Much can change in eleven years."

"I know," she mumbled, thinking of all the changes life had wrought in her.

"But I don't think a person's entire moral compass can change so drastically, not really. So, I'm asking you, Sebastian, honestly, how sure are we that this intel on him is correct?"

"You saw the picture, Bella, it was him."

Sebastian lifted his head from the report he was scrutinising to survey her with sympathetic understanding.

"I'm sorry, but there's no doubt. Nick Eastman is in bed with some very bad people indeed."

"And now he's in my bed," Isabella muttered, her skin crawling at the thought.

~Chapter Six~
"It's so hard not to touch you, Isabella."

Taking the next day off to get some much-needed rest, Isabella deliberately ignored the three calls that came from Nick and didn't read any of his four texts. She would see him tomorrow. Now she wanted some time off to think about the situation and clear her head ready to face him again.

Looking for a distraction, she turned the music up to full blast and cleaned her house from top to bottom. Getting into the rhythm of the pounding beat, she worked up a sweat with a bout of cathartic extreme housework which, in her reasoning, was as good as a workout at the gym and had the added benefit of leaving her with a clean house.

Finally taking pity on her neighbours she turned it off and the sudden silence was pierced with the prolonged ringing of the doorbell. Her heart stood still. Isabella wondered if it was Nick, if her radio silence had forced him to come in person. She cursed herself for ever inviting him to her home.

Cautiously, she approached the front door, studying the shadowy figure visible through the opaque glass. No, unless Nick had managed to shrink a good foot and suddenly sprout long dark hair, it wasn't him.

Isabella opened the door and startled Kit in the act of raising her finger to the bell again.

"Oh," gasped Kit in surprise. "You *are* in. I heard the music and guessed you must be but couldn't make you hear the bell."

"Sorry," panted Isabella. "But I was cleaning, and I find the music helps to keep me going. Come in, what can I do for you?"

"Thank you." Kit stepped into the hallway, her eyes looking around with unabashed curiosity. "Susannah told me to come, she said that you would be the best person to help me."

"Help you with what?"

"Learning self-defence."

"I see. Why do you feel you need to learn?"

"I travel a lot with the company. We're always in one city or another, and last week I was in Vienna. A friend of mine, one of the young girls from the ensemble, went out to grab a late-night meal. She didn't go into the bad part of the city – we all know to avoid those areas because, trust me, every city has a bad area – but she was mugged all the same. Luckily, he only stole her bag and slapped her about a bit. But it could have been worse, much worse, and it could have happened to me. So, I want to learn how to protect myself, and others if I must."

Isabella nodded slowly, looking at the clothes Kit was wearing. Loose cotton summer trousers and a baggy tee-shirt.

"Fine," she said. "Dump your bag and shoes here, take off any jewellery and follow me."

Bemused, Kit did as she said, and followed Isabella upstairs to the third bedroom, which

Isabella had kitted out as a mini gym and workout room. Pulling padded mats from a stack against one wall, Isabella laid them out on the floor and then turned to look at Kit.

"Right, let's see what you're made of, and then we'll know where we have to begin."

"Thank you…" Kit began.

"Oh, don't thank me," Isabella grinned. "By the time I've finished with you, you're going to hate me."

Whilst she might not have hated her, by the time Isabella called a halt for the day and Kit had left, bruised, and shaking, she must have been seriously regretting her visit.

Although flexible, the young woman was soft and reluctant to fight back. Like most women, the urge to not hurt anyone was engrained deep, and most of their session had been Isabella patiently picking apart that attitude.

Sometimes, she pointed out to Kit, a woman needed to want to hurt. And, once that decision had been made, then a woman had to have the courage of her convictions and the skill to carry it through. If you are being attacked, she explained, you can be damned sure your attacker won't have any qualms about hurting or even killing you. So, you must be prepared to meet force with force.

Kit, to her credit, had listened and tried. Gradually, throughout the session, she got tougher, and by the end, Isabella was confident she would be able to make something of the younger woman. At least giving her the ability to defend herself, if necessary.

Watching as a sweat-drenched Kit thankfully gulped at her water, Isabella frowned when she broke off coughing violently.

"Steady," she laughed, as Kit turned red and struggled to breathe.

"Sorry," Kit gasped. "I've had a sore throat for a couple of days, and sometimes it seems to flare up in a spasm."

"That's surely not good for an opera singer?" Isabella frowned.

"It's not," Kit agreed, and pulled a face. "Perils of the job, I'm afraid. I have a few days to rest, well, I'm singing at a friend's funeral tomorrow. But just one song, and then I can rest."

"I'm sorry. "Was she a good friend?"

"Yes," Kit's expression fell. "The best. Annaliese Macleod. She was the one who helped me get started. I owe her everything."

"The author?" asked Isabella and Kit nodded. "I heard on the news about her death. I thought how sad it was, she was so young and lovely. Brain tumour, right?"

"Yes, by the time it was diagnosed there was nothing that could be done about it, and then she was gone, and it's such a shame..."

Kit broke off in another fit of coughing, and Isabella silently offered her a box of tissues.

"Rest your voice," she said. "It's too precious to mess about with, and if it doesn't get any better then go and see a doctor."

Wednesday came all too soon. Donning her IT consultant clothes and carrying her laptop and the tricks of her trade in a bag slung over her shoulder, Isabella pushed open the door of Corlux and once again strode up to Karen the PA, who this time was smiling at her in approval of an appointment made.

"Mr Eastman told me to expect you, Ms Santorini, and that you're going to sort out our computer system," she said, once Isabella was close enough to talk to.

"Well, I'm going to try." Isabella smiled, and then glanced at the shut office door. "Do I need to see Mr Eastman first? Or have you somewhere I can set up?"

"I cleared a desk for you," Karen told her and gestured to the nearest cubicle where a flat empty surface beckoned.

Smiling, Isabella unpacked her bag onto the desk – well, all the things that she was happy with anyone seeing, she unpacked. The tools of her *other* trade were secreted away on various parts of her person.

Isabella only hoped she would have a chance to deploy them but, glancing around the crowded room, she was unsure if that would be possible.

But then, she had been in situations like this before, learning that so long as she acted like what she was doing was entirely above board and normal, people would completely ignore her.

As she plugged in her laptop, she heard the office door open behind her, and knew without turning around, that he was there.

"Ah, Isabella. Could I have a word please?"

"Of course," she murmured. Fixing a polite smile on her face she walked past Nick into his office, waiting as he closed the door.

"Isabella," he breathed, then he was upon her, and her back was pressed up against the solid wood of the door and his lips were on hers, and she ... damn it, she couldn't resist him, and she was kissing him back.

His hands roved over her body and Isabella knew she needed to stop him because he was the enemy, and she was here to use him and expose him, but oh ... how could she fight against a large strong hand that was pushing her skirt upwards and finding the very core of her.

"Nick," she gasped.

"I missed you yesterday," he murmured. "I called and texted, but you never answered."

"I had company," she replied honestly.

"Company?" Her heart lurched at the almost jealousy in his voice.

"Yes, my sister-in-law."

"Oh." Then he was unbuttoning her shirt, his hands skimming the lace underneath.

"Nick, stop." From somewhere she dredged up the strength to push him away and refasten her buttons. "Not here, not now."

He hesitated, and she watched in fascination as he visibly struggled to regain control of his senses. Running a shaking hand over his face, he stepped back and gave her space.

"You're right, I'm sorry. You're here to do a job, and I shouldn't ... but it's so hard not to touch you, Isabella. I've thought about nothing but you since the weekend. I want to see you again, outside of office hours."

She nodded, glad of the solid support of the door as her legs did that turning to jelly thing again. He's bad, her head was screaming at her. So very, very bad. What he does, who he's working for, he destroys so many lives.

I don't care, pouted her heart, and now her body was in league with it, craving him, needing his touch. She took a deep breath.

"Whilst we're at work we must maintain a professional attitude at all times."

"And when we're not at work?"

"I … I want to be with you."

It's for the sake of the mission, Isabella's head told her. Yeah right, her heart sniggered at her self-delusion. You keep telling yourself that if it makes you feel better.

Isabella worked conspicuously hard all day, only stopping to exchange a few words with Karen when the ever-efficient PA kindly brought her a sandwich and a coffee at lunchtime.

Working her way around the antiquated system, Isabella made notes and tinkered, clearing obsolete data that was cluttering and slowing down the run time.

She genuinely knew more than the average person about computers due to extensive courses she had attended, and any extra help she needed was ably provided by Seamus muttering in her ear.

Planting the shadowing malware had been laughably easy. After the initial few minutes of interest, everyone settled down to their tasks and ignored her. Hooking up her laptop to the office system and introducing her own s*pecial* software under the guise of "checking" their run time, had the employee on the next desk nodding as Isabella spouted technobabble at him.

Finally, as the day began to close, Isabella packed all her toys away and went to tap on

Nick's door that had remained resolutely closed the whole time.

"I've done as much as I can," she told him after he bid her come in and she shut the door behind her. "I've cleaned up your system – you really should tell your staff to empty their bins a bit more often, and maybe quit playing quite so much candy crush in their spare time – so that should speed things up a bit. I've run a scan disk and have tidied up your files."

"Will that solve all our problems?"

"No, it will help speed you up a bit, but unfortunately the system you're using simply isn't man enough for what you're asking it to do. It probably was enough when the company started, but as you've expanded it's putting more and more of a drain on it, which is slowing it down and causing the glitches." She took a deep breath and gave him a wry smile.

"Unfortunately, all I can recommend is a completely new system – one designed to cope with the company's current needs."

Nick slowly nodded as he digested her report.

"Thank you, at least now we know what needs to be done. If you get your company to bill us, I'll see it's settled immediately."

"I will," Isabella turned to go.

"Isabella."

"Yes?"

"Tonight."

"Yes."

~Chapter Seven~
"I want you to remember us this way."

Reaching the base, Isabella went straight to see Seamus and discovered him and Sebastian frowning in mutual disbelief over a bank of computers.

"Problem?" she asked, picking up on the vibe in the room immediately.

"A mystery," Sebastian replied and nodded towards Seamus. "Tell her."

"We can't find anything within their system," his soft Irish accent sounded perplexed as Seamus wrinkled his brow at her.

"Nothing?" Isabella dumped her laptop bag on the desk and went to stand behind them, gazing at the information processing and whirling on the screens. "There must be something."

"If there is, it's buried so deep behind firewalls that even I can't get to it, but I don't think this old system could support such a sophisticated setup. I mean," he threw his hand up in despair at the screen. "This system was old five years ago, now it's positively antique. It just doesn't make sense."

"It would if the company is just a front," Sebastian said. "Perhaps they don't need to waste money on state-of-the-art equipment, because this isn't the system, they run their real business on."

"Maybe," Seamus agreed, then took his glasses off and rubbed a hand across gritty eyes.

"Take a break," Sebastian ordered. "Come at it fresh in the morning. You've both been looking at screens all day, so have a break."

"Sure." Seamus stretched in his chair and looked at Isabella. "Drink?" he offered hopefully.

Isabella smiled gently at the diminutive Irishman. That Seamus had a "thing" for his boss was common knowledge about the base. That Isabella would never do anything about it was common knowledge to everyone but Seamus.

"I'm sorry, I can't," she said. "I have a work assignment tonight," and she looked directly at Sebastian who had the grace to look slightly ashamed.

"Be careful," he told her.

"I always am," she replied grimly.

Dinner, in a warm and inviting Italian restaurant just off Kensington High Street, felt like coming home, and Isabella relaxed enough to speak Italian to the waiter.

His face lighting up, he fetched the owner who smiled and laughed as he chatted to Isabella about which part of Italy she was from, and whether she knew his nephew, Luigi, who ran a restaurant in the same town?

Nick raised his brows at her as a fresh plate of appetisers were placed on the table between them – "on the house" – and a carafe of house red was expertly poured into their oversized glasses.

"How to make yourself popular," he murmured, as they touched glasses.

"It's nice to speak to people from home sometimes," Isabella replied and took an approving sip of the rich, full-bodied wine.

"Have you ever been back?" he asked in interest.

"I was in Italy a few months ago on a job, but I didn't go back home – there's nothing there for me now. The house was sold years ago, and I have no family in the area anymore." She paused to sip thoughtfully at her wine.

"That's a good thing about my job. I do a lot of travelling with it, which I love. I always enjoy seeing new parts of the world."

"I remember," Nick mused. "All those plans we made to travel together, to go everywhere, and…"

"See everything …" Isabella finished the sentence, and they exchanged a nostalgic smile, in that instant transported back to the boy and the girl they had been, so long ago.

"So, how about you?" she continued. "Have you travelled much?"

"Well, I've seen pretty much all the States, and most of Europe. I had a long holiday out in Australia about five years ago, and a trip to Shanghai – which was interesting."

"How about the Middle East?" Isabella asked casually.

"No," he said. "I've never been there."

He was lying. She knew he was. Not just because Sebastian had shown her further photographs of Nick in Kandahar, but also because her senses told her he was.

"How about you?" he asked. "Have you ever been there?"

"No," she smoothly lied. "It's not exactly known for its enlightened attitude towards women. I think if ever my company had a contract out there, they'd probably send one of my male colleagues.

He nodded thoughtfully, and then their food arrived, and they relaxed into the evening, the untruths lying between them on the table along with the garlic bread and olive oil.

She went back to his hotel with him. Even if the mission had not required it, she still would have done. She had even slipped some toiletry essentials into her capacious bag.

Once more riding up in the elevator in total silence, when they reached the sanctuary of his room and he turned to her, the brief thought dashed through her mind that she should leave – now – get away while she still could.

But then he said her name and his hands were upon her, and even if she'd been told he was the devil himself, Isabella would have been powerless to make herself leave.

Afterwards, in the glow of complete and utter satisfaction, she lay in his arms. Her heart breaking at the thought of what she knew must come, still, she breathed in the scent of his skin as if committing it to memory.

"Isabella." He looked at the dark head lying on his chest. "There's something I must tell you."

"What?" She raised her face to his, saw the seriousness of his expression and swiftly pulled herself up to sit beside him, the sheet clutched across her chest. "What is it?"

"Well, I must tell you two things. Firstly, I won't be able to see you for a few days."

"Oh?"

"I'm going away on a business trip, only to Brussels, but it's a tricky situation and I may be gone more than a few days."

"And the other thing?"

"I love you. I wanted to tell you that before I left, just in case."

"In case of what?"

"Oh, I don't know. It's just, stuff happens, and you wish you'd said things when you had the chance."

"What do you think is going to happen to you in Brussels?"

"Other than me dying of boredom in endless pointless meetings, you mean?" He grinned at her but quickly became serious again.

"I wanted you to know how I felt, I wanted you to know that I love you, Isabella Santorini. Always have, always will. And that you must trust me."

"Trust you?" Isabella stared at him in surprise, her thoughts in a whirl. It was almost as if he was...

"Yes, trust me. Whatever happens, I want you to remember us this way, and remember that I love you, so much."

"Nick, you're scaring me. Are you mixed up in something? Something, I don't know, something dangerous?"

There, she had given him a chance to tell her, given an opportunity to confess to her himself precisely what kind of man he had become.

For a moment he looked at her, and it was as if a strange man looked from his eyes, a man on the edge of all reason and sanity. Then he smiled, the look vanished, and he was just Nick again.

"No, of course not," he laughed, and his hands slid to her shoulders, gently pushing the sheet down to touch and caress in the way he knew she liked.

"Ignore me," he murmured. "I'm just being silly. It's being with you once more – I think it's addled my senses, made me a stupid teenager again."

"Nick," she protested, wanting him to talk to her some more, somehow feeling he had been on the verge of confessing everything.

But did she want him to? Or did she want him to stay silent so she could enjoy the charade for a little while longer? Pretend that they were who they appeared to be, two people enjoying a rekindled love affair.

"I love you," she murmured, suddenly desperate to say it at least once more.

"I love you too," he whispered.

They were the words she wanted him to say, but why did it feel like he was saying goodbye.

At work the next day, Isabella reported in private to Sebastian all that occurred the previous evening, unwilling to have the rest of the team know how close she was getting to the suspect.

She knew that the surveillance team would be aware she was spending nights with him, but still, they didn't have to hear all the gory details.

When she finished, Sebastian was silent for a few minutes. Looking at his hands, he appeared lost in thought.

"He told you he was going to Brussels?" he finally asked, and Isabella nodded.

"Yes."

"Did you believe him?"

"Maybe," she shrugged.

"Isabella, Nick Eastman boarded a flight to Afghanistan at 7:27 this morning."

Isabella looked away from the sympathy in her cousin's eyes. She left Nick's hotel room at six, so he must have gone to the airport as soon as she left his bed. It hurt, the lies and the deception. Even though she had known, had been prepared for it, still ... it hurt.

"I see," was all she said though. "What are we doing about that?"

"He was followed, and our agents in Afghanistan have been alerted. If he meets with The Preacher, we will know about it."

"So, is that it then? Is my part over?"

"I don't know. If he doesn't meet with The Preacher for some reason, or our agents are unable to follow him when he comes back to the UK, then we will need you to pick up where you left off."

"And if they do catch him, what happens to Nick then?"

"You know the answer to that one, Isabella.

He was right, she did. Terrorism, treason, drug smuggling – these were all serious offences. If Nick were caught and convicted of even one of them, he would go away for a very long time and she would never see him again – not that she wanted to, her head hastily added.

She went home. Spent the next few days going about her life as normal. Yet, nothing was normal. Mechanically, she did her job – the Ricci case needed writing up, other ongoing missions demanded her attention. There was paperwork and correspondence to catch up on.

Isabella dealt with them all, only a part of her present, the rest of her in Afghanistan, wondering about Nick – where he was and what he was doing. Wondering if he was thinking of her, as he effectively destroyed any chance, they may have had of being together.

Most of all, she wondered what could have gone so very wrong in his life to have warped the idealistic and honourable boy she had known into the amoral man he had allegedly become.

She continued to train Kit. Pleased with how well the younger woman was coming along, she was concerned about the persistent cough that didn't seem to heal, and gently pressed her to see a doctor.

And all the time she thought about Nick, about the way it had been between them, unable to believe something that had felt so very right, could be so very wrong.

~Chapter Eight~
"You better hope she wakes up."

Five days slipped by with no word from Nick. The agent following him and those in Afghanistan reported his arrival in the country. He had landed at the airport and taken a taxi to a hotel in the middle of the city.

For two days, agents watched the hotel, with no sign of him, then on the third slipped the porter a bribe to open his room for them. They discovered a room completely devoid of any sign he had been there at all.

Somehow, he knew he was being followed and gave them the slip, and this evidence of familiarity with stealth and secrecy further hammered a nail in his coffin.

Isabella knew what he was, the proof was irrefutable, and she derided herself as a fool for even daring to hope otherwise.

Sadness gripped her heart. It would have been better, she told herself fiercely, to have never met him again, to have retained the beautiful memory of their affair as an ideal and unsullied recollection.

Now ... now it was besmirched and splattered with the innocent blood of those he must have caused misery and death to, and Isabella mourned his loss all over again.

Unable to sleep at night, her body twitched with unsatisfied desire for him, remembering the feel of his touch; how gentle he had been with her, how he had instinctively known how to please her.

And her mind returned constantly to the memory of their last night together, of his face when he asked her to trust him, and her heart ached at his deception.

On the sixth day, she received a text from him. Stark and simple, it merely said – meet me, please, 9pm, tell no one – and gave the name of a popular bar in central London.

She considered the message.

Her head knew she should alert her team, at the very least tell Sebastian, but she hesitated...

As far as she knew, he was unaware Nick was back in the UK. At least, if Sebastian did know, he hadn't seen fit to inform her. She considered that, as well. Would Sebastian keep such a thing from her?

Maybe, she reluctantly decided, to protect her. If they no longer needed her to complete the mission, he would cut her out of the loop without compunction.

Isabella read the message again.

She needed to see him, alone.

She had to talk to him, to find out for herself what happened to him.

Once she had answers, she would bring him in herself, and let whatever authority wanted Nick Eastman the most, have him. But Isabella wanted one last chance to speak with him.

"Okay."

She texted the single word back, and almost instantly regretted it. Yet she knew when 9pm came, she would be sitting in that bar waiting for the man who had broken her heart for a second time.

Only this time, she had let him do it.

It was a nice bar, sophisticated and quiet. At 9pm on a mid-week evening, the clientele was sparse, and Isabella had no trouble slipping into an empty booth with a view of the bar and the door.

She waited.

Her heart thumping with sick anticipation, she waited. She watched the door as 9pm came and went with no sign of him.

She waited until twenty minutes past the hour, ramrod stiff in her seat, an untouched whisky before her.

Fingers idly toying with the locket she had not removed since Nick had once again placed it around her neck, she felt the eyes of the barman upon her.

He thinks I've been stood up, she thought. *He's not wrong*, she wryly agreed. Rising to her feet, she angrily pulled her leather jacket on and picked up her bag.

Enough games.

She was leaving.

In the morning she would go to Sebastian and confess everything. They would try to trace where the message had come from – although she had a feeling, they would be unsuccessful – and that would be an end to this stupid situation.

Nick Eastman would be consigned to history, and she would never think of him again.

Liar sneered her heart.

Okay, she would try never to think of him again, she amended crossly. Striding to the door, and yanking it open, she emerged into the cool of a London evening.

She had parked her car in a side street a few yards down and set off, keys in hand. Home, she wanted to be home. Maybe take a long hot bath and then something mindless on TV.

Yes ... that was the plan.

"Isabella."

At the sound of her name being hissed from a darkened doorway, she hesitated. It sounded like...

"Nick?" she asked.

A hand gestured to her in the gloom, and she stepped cautiously towards the figure she could barely make out there.

"Nick?" she asked again.

She was closer now and could see it wasn't him. The dark features and eyes of the man standing there were nothing like Nick's and she moved swiftly back in an abrupt and acute awareness of danger.

"Who are you?" she snapped.

"We have a mutual friend," he said, stepping from the shadows to reveal the Middle Eastern cast to his features.

"Who?" she asked, still unafraid because there was no man Isabella Santorini couldn't best in a fair fight.

There was a screech of tires behind her, and a van mounted the pavement. She turned to run but there were too many of them in the way, so she had to fight.

She took three of them down with her before they finally tackled her to the ground, kicking and punching her into submission.

Still struggling desperately, she roared in angry frustration as one yanked up the sleeve of her jacket and a hypodermic needle glistened in the light of the nearby streetlamp.

"Let me go," she screamed, and managed to kick the one holding the needle, so it dropped to the ground.

Wrenching her arm free, she punched her way up out of the melee and managed a step, before the back of her jacket was grabbed and she was forced to the ground, her legs kicked out from under her, and the sharp sting of the needle was in her neck.

She felt the coldness enter her veins. Tried to fight the numbing blackness but it was too much for her and she slumped forward in the arms of her captors.

"Throw her in the van, quick," she dimly heard one of them say, and then the tide pulled her under, and she knew no more.

Vague images floated behind her eyelids as Isabella struggled to wake up. Each time, the darkness pulled her back and she succumbed.

"For fuck's sake," she heard an irritated male voice exclaim from a million miles away. "How much did you give her?"

"Bitch wouldn't go down," another male voice muttered sourly.

"Well, you better hope she wakes up before we get there," the first voice remonstrated. "She'll be no good to The Preacher dead or unconscious."

The Preacher…

Why did that name mean something to her? Isabella struggled to think, to remember, but her brains turned sluggishly in her skull, and it was all too much, so she gratefully let sleep claim her.

Daylight. She could feel daylight on her face, and a hard stone surface beneath her body. As Isabella Santorini awoke for good this time and cautiously cranked her eyelids open, she became aware of several things simultaneously.

She was lying on the hard stone floor of a small and sparsely furnished cell. The sunlight she could feel was coming from a tiny, barred window set into the rocky ceiling high above her head.

There were stout bars to her left, and thick rock walls all around.

Her body was one big mass of hurt. Tentatively, she tried to move. Severe bruising, everywhere. Her ribs hurt. She took a deep breath, they ached but there was no stabbing pain inside, so she didn't think they were broken.

Also, her bladder was full, achingly full.

Looking around the cell, she spotted a bucket in one corner intended for that purpose and dragged herself over to it to address that need at least.

There was a rough cot in one corner, with a thin pillow and an even thinner mattress. Stumbling to it, Isabella sank gratefully onto it. Hard as iron, it was still more comfortable than the floor.

There was movement at the barred door and Isabella quickly glanced up to see a woman standing there holding a tray. Two men with guns flanked her and one reached over to unlock the cell door to allow the woman to enter.

The door clanged shut behind her, and the woman visibly flinched as she crossed to Isabella with the tray.

Brown eyes briefly met Isabella's over the dark material of her chador, and then looked down at the tray.

"Please," the woman said, her voice soft and low, her English stilted. "I bring you food and water. You eat now."

"Thank you," Isabella said, and reached for the tray, frowning at the terror that leapt into the woman's eyes.

"It's all right," Isabella said, spreading her hands wide. "I won't hurt you."

The woman gave one quick scared nod, then thrust the tray into Isabella's hands and scuttled back to the door.

The men unlocked it for her and muttered something to her that had the woman glancing back at Isabella with something akin to pity in her eyes, before disappearing into the darkness of the corridor that wound away from the cell.

Looking her up and down contemptuously, the two men followed her. Left alone again, Isabella surveyed the contents of the tray with interest.

She had recognised the language the men spoke as Afghanistan, the chador the woman wore on her head was the typical native dress of that country, and the dish of qormah and dumplings on the tray were traditional food.

Afghanistan, she was in Afghanistan then.

Thirstily, Isabella drank deeply from the earthenware jug of water, then ate the food hungrily. It was good, much better than would be given to a person they intended to kill.

And anyway, she reasoned. Why bring her all the way here just to kill her? She had been outnumbered on the street, one swift slice with a blade or a bullet to the back of her head would have got the job done. So, why go to all the trouble of drugging her and smuggling her into Afghanistan?

No, Isabella concluded. She was needed here, alive, for some reason. Something to do with The Preacher, she presumed. He was the only connection she had with Afghanistan apart from Nick Eastman.

Nick, her thoughts faltered. Was he responsible for her abduction? Was this all some sick plan he had?

The woman had left a packet of hand wipes, some tissues and antiseptic lotion on the tray, and thankfully Isabella wiped down the bits of her she could reach. Smearing the antiseptic onto her various cuts and scrapes, she wondered if her disappearance had been discovered yet.

That thought had her reaching in her jacket pocket for her phone, but of course, it was gone.

~Chapter Nine~
"She was a bit of fun."

They left her waiting all that day and for much of the next before finally they took her from her cell at gunpoint and forced her to walk down endless stone passageways to where The Preacher awaited her.

During those days, the same woman had brought her two more trays of food, and hot water to wash. She had also emptied the bucket.

Both times, Isabella spoke softly and politely to her. Thanking her for the food and her attention, Isabella fancied the looks the woman shot her way were altogether kindlier, even pitying.

And now she was standing in a large cavern, with bright, overhead lights casting long spiky shadows away into the gloomy corners.

Isabella was sensible enough to doubt her chances of getting out of this alive, but at the same time, this was what she had trained for all those years. Furthermore, her pride would not let them see her fear.

Head held high, she had set the pace and refused to allow her armed escort to hurry her until finally, they were walking at her speed.

This tiny victory gave her the further courage to straighten her spine and lift her chin as she was led towards a crude rocky dais at one end of the cavern where a man stood, waiting for her.

He was tall and corpulent, fleshy jowls crinkled as his swarthy complexion moved upwards into a smile of such insincere welcome that something shivered deep within Isabella, and she knew she was face to face with pure evil.

Over the years, Isabella had met men who committed heinous crimes. Men, and even the odd woman, who had done things so bad they didn't bear thinking about, and she realised they all divided into two groups.

For some, it was purely about personal gain. That in the pursuit of their own selfish needs, they didn't much care if anyone else got hurt or even killed. Yet, they wouldn't go out of their way to inflict pain if it served no purpose.

Those individuals were easier to understand, and their actions could even be predicted. Once they were cornered and there was no way out, then they would instantly try to cut a deal, to make things as easy for themselves as possible.

Then there was the second group – those for whom bloodletting and pain was a sport, a game that titivated and entertained.

Thinking nothing of destroying a whole community simply because they could, they were unpredictable and much more dangerous, liable to go down in a blaze of glory when cornered rather than do the sensible thing. They would never admit defeat and look for ways to soften the blow.

Instead, they would rather die and usually weren't too bothered about whom they took down with them.

Looking into the dark eyes of the man known only as The Preacher, Isabella recognised that he was of the second group and her heart sank.

There would be no reasoning with him, no appealing to his better nature because he was without one.

She stopped and faced him, her eyes remaining fixed on his. Calmly and dispassionately, she studied him, until at last, he glanced away, and she allowed a tiny smile to play across her face.

"Who are you?" she demanded indignantly. "Why have I been kidnapped? Where am I? I am a British citizen, I have rights, and I demand that you let me go."

One of her guards stepped closer, raising his gun, and barking something at her in his language.

When she shook her head in confusion, he pushed the end of his gun into her temple – forcing her to her knees and watching as The Preacher stepped down from the dais and paced to loom over her.

"Rights? No, Miss Santorini, I am afraid you have no rights here."

"What do you want from me?" she snapped, pushing away the gun with her hand and staring angrily up at The Preacher.

"You are the woman of Nick Eastman. We have been watching you. You have been spending much time with him."

"Nick?"

Isabella allowed the surprise to be obvious in her voice as she continued.

"This is all because of Nick?"

"What do you know of Nick Eastman, Miss Santorini? How well do you know the man whose bed you have been sharing?"

"We knew each other a long time ago in Italy," Isabella said.

Seeing no reason to lie and not knowing what Nick might have already told them, she chose to stick to the truth – for now.

"Childhood sweethearts, is that what you want me to believe?"

"It's the truth," Isabella shrugged. "We had a relationship, it ended, the way holiday romances do, and until last week I had neither seen nor heard from him in over a decade."

"Until you met again and decided to see if old flames could be rekindled?"

The man's English was impeccable, and Isabella wondered if he'd had a British university education.

"Yes, that's about it."

"So, you would say Nick Eastman has a fondness for you. That he would be unwilling to see any harm come to you."

"I ... I hope so."

Isabella suddenly had a nasty suspicion where this was going.

"Shall we put that to the test?"

The Preacher leaned closer, his eyes glittering with malicious intent and Isabella flinched from his bad breath and the madness that flickered in the pitch depths of his eyes.

Then he smiled again, and it was a smile of spiteful power, the smile of someone who took delight in the suffering of others.

He barked an order to one of the guards, who turned and left the cavern without saying anything.

The Preacher returned to the dais, and Isabella shakily rose to her feet, eyeing her guards as she did so.

They leered at her, and one stroked his gun suggestively, but neither made a move to stop her and she wondered if this had all been planned out in advance – a series of coldly calculated moves to frighten her into submission.

Isabella would go along with their little act, for now, but was confident they had no idea who, or rather what, she was. She would bide her time and await an opportunity to escape.

Long minutes ticked by, then there was movement at one of the entrances to the cavern and Nick was there.

Striding into the large space he went first to the dais and bowed his head respectfully to the figure standing there.

"You sent for me," he said, and The Preacher nodded.

"I did, I have someone I want you to meet," and he gestured with his hand towards Isabella.

Nick turned.

His eyes met hers.

She saw sudden shock and horrified dismay before the shutters came down and he turned to The Preacher in apparent irritation.

"What the hell is this all about?"

"I thought you might be missing your woman, so I arranged for her to be brought to you," The Preacher oozed.

"My woman? Her?"

Nick dismissed the idea with a contemptuous shrug of his shoulders.

"She's not my woman. She was a bit of fun, a way to pass the time."

"And that is all?"

"Sure, I had an itch, I scratched it. Western women are a lot looser than those of your country. A man doesn't have to marry them to get between their legs."

There was a low appreciative chuckle amongst those of the other men who understood enough English to get his meaning.

Isabella swallowed down her rage.

Later.

There would be time for killing him later. First, she had to get out of there alive.

"Nick?" she allowed wounded bewilderment to creep into her voice. "What are you saying? I ... I thought you loved me?"

"Love you?" Nick snorted with amusement. "You were a distraction, a bit of fun, a good lay."

With each word he stepped closer until they were face to face, staring into each other's eyes.

Isabella met his hazel gaze, unable to tell if it was a desperate act to convince them of her unimportance to him.

Or if it were the truth.

"If she truly means nothing to you, then you will not care what happens to her."

The Preacher's words cut through their silent scrutiny of one another.

"You will not care if I make a gift of her to my men ..."

There was a swell in the testosterone levels within the cavern, as every man surveyed her with lusty interest.

"After all, if she is as good as you claim, then why shouldn't they all have a taste?"

Nick shot The Preacher an angry look.

"I don't share my toys," he snapped and grabbed Isabella by the arm. "And now you have so thoughtfully brought her to me, I intend to have lots of playtime."

Isabella angrily yanked her arm away and slapped him as hard as she could around the face.

"Bastard," she cried. "Keep your hands off me."

Nick rubbed at his face where the marks of her hand could be seen, then grinned ruefully at the other men as they chuckled at him.

"I do not think playtime will be as pleasant as it was," The Preacher drawled. "Unless you are the kind of man who enjoys taking by force. No, I have a much better idea."

"Oh?" Nick looked warily at his master. "What's that?"

"There have been certain … concerns … raised about your loyalty," The Preacher replied blandly. "Your sudden conversion to our cause, your rapid rise to power – it all seems a little too convenient – and many have questioned your true motives."

"You know I am loyal to you," Nick snapped angrily.

"Show me these men who would accuse me," he demanded. "And I will show you jealous fools who lack the courage and the brains to serve you the way I do."

"Nevertheless," The Preacher continued as if Nick hadn't spoken. "Enough whispers have come to my ears that I too am … shall we say –

curious – as to how deeply your commitment runs."

"How can I prove it to you?" Nick demanded, and The Preacher paused as if considering the question.

"There is one way."

"Name it."

"Take your woman outside and put a bullet through her beautiful face. Then your loyalty will be beyond question."

~Chapter Ten~
"Wait for the signal,"

Silence fell over the cavern, and Isabella watched as Nick's back stiffened almost imperceptibly. Then he shrugged and turned to grip her arm again, his fingers closing like steel vices around her flesh.

"No problem," he snarled and pulled a handgun from the waistband of his jeans.

"Move," he growled at Isabella and began dragging her towards one of the exits.

"Wait." The Preacher held up a languid hand. "Badih will go with you, just to make sure the job gets done."

He nodded to one of Isabella's guards, who grinned nastily and followed them, chuckling as Nick yanked Isabella so viciously, she stumbled and almost fell, clutching at the rocky wall to stop herself from sprawling at his feet.

He murmured something in his native language to Nick, who paused impatiently and gave Isabella a look of irritated exasperation, that – if real – made her want to punch the smirk from his face.

But the gun he held to her ribs was real enough, as was the one loosely trained on her by Badih, so she swallowed down her anger, her mind desperately running through her options.

Outside, bright sunlight hit them in the face and Isabella squinted as she was dragged across the rocky sand to where an outcrop of cliff formed a natural small canyon.

Old rusty stains of blood were splattered over its walls and on the ground and Isabella swallowed, knowing full well what it was – an execution yard.

"Nick."

She tried to look him in the eye.

"Shut up," he ordered and threw her roughly to the ground.

Badih moved over to pull her up, his hands running over her body, his breath quickening with obvious arousal and his eyes making his intentions clear.

Looking over his shoulder, he said something to Nick. Isabella didn't need to understand to know exactly what he was asking.

He wanted to have some fun with her before Nick put a bullet in her brain, and Isabella pushed him away in disgust.

Nick rolled his eyes.

"Put her down, Badih," he ordered in English. "Let's get this done so I can get on with my work."

Disappointed, Badih regretfully let Isabella go and stepped away.

"Nick," she began again, unable to believe he was going to do this. "Nick, please…"

"I said, shut up," he snapped, and raised his gun and fired.

The shot echoed around the enclosed canyon. At point-blank range, he couldn't have missed, and Nick hadn't.

Her eyes wide with shock and her heart thudding in her chest, Isabella looked at the perfect hole in the centre of Badih's forehead, as he slumped to the ground – his face frozen in an expression of eternal surprise.

Then Nick was pulling her into his arms, his body damp with adrenalin induced sweat and his heart pounding so fiercely she could feel it through his shirt.

"Oh, my god," he muttered. "Isabella," and he kissed her, then stepped back.

"Punch me," he ordered.

"What?"

"I said, punch me – hard."

"Why?"

"I can't exactly go back to them with my hair combed, not if I want to convince them you managed to get the jump on me, took my gun, shot Badih and made off into the desert before I could stop you."

"They'll never believe that." Isabella cried, taking the gun he gave her and tucking it into her jacket. "Come with me."

"I can't."

"Why not?"

"I just can't ... it's complicated, Isabella. I wish I had time to explain, but you need to go."

"Where?"

"Follow this outcrop, a few yards down there is the goat shelter. Hide in there. When it's dark I'll come and get you. They'll never think to look for you there, they'll expect you to try and get away."

"But..."

"There's no time, Isabella. Now, hit me."

So, she did. Ploughing all her fear, rage, and pent-up anger into one almighty punch, she hit him on the jaw and had the satisfaction of seeing him stagger back and almost fall.

Shocked, he spat blood out onto the ground and rubbed at his rapidly bruising chin.

"You punch good," he muttered. "For a girl."

"Want me to hit you again," Isabella snarled, and raised her clenched fist.

"No, no, we're good." Hastily he held up his hands to ward her off, then his expression softened as he stared at her.

The moment hung between them, and Isabella swallowed, knowing there was a strong chance this was the last time she would ever see him.

"Nick..."

"Don't ..." he replied, then held her to him and kissed her softly. "Wait until a little past nightfall. If I haven't come for you then head out in that direction." He pointed out into the desert.

"Follow the trail, try not to get caught, and a couple of hours hard walking will get you to Kandahar. Go to the British embassy, they'll help you get home."

"But Nick, you..."

"Don't wait for me, Isabella. If I haven't come for you by then, it's because something has stopped me, so I need to know that you won't do anything stupid. You have no idea what these men are capable of, and I'm sorry I got you mixed up in all this."

Then he looked at her one more time, with a world of regret and goodbye in his eyes and walked away from her.

Crouching low, she ran to the goat shed which was little more than a rough lean-to fastened to the cliff wall.

Working her way into the shadows at the back, Isabella found an old pile of sacks and squirmed down in between them and settled down to wait.

Her mind in a whirl, she thought about Nick. He was in this up to his neck, yet, he had risked everything by not killing her as ordered.

Isabella thought about The Preacher, about his eyes as he'd stared into hers. He would not be easy to fool, and she prayed Nick was convincing enough. If he wasn't...

If he wasn't ... Isabella knew The Preacher wouldn't hesitate to shoot him where he stood, and then come after her.

Minutes ticked by, then she heard shouting and engines revving up. Softly, she moved within the sacks to press her eye to a small chink in the uneven planking of the wall.

Men were rushing around the compound, jumping into the vehicles that were parked there and roaring off into the desert.

At least that part of Nick's tale they had believed. Then she froze at the sound of voices right outside the shelter.

A man – he was talking to someone else who was standing in the entrance to the shelter. Hardly daring to breathe, Isabella waited.

The other person replied, her voice low and concerned. It was the woman who had brought her food. She was coming into the shelter, walking to the very back. She bent to grasp a sack of something from the corner and the man's voice lifted in an enquiry.

The woman looked around and her eyes locked with Isabella's.

For a beat, the two women from opposite ends of the world gazed at one another. Then the woman turned to the man who had stepped into the shelter. Waving him away as if dismissing his offer of help, she followed him out.

They stood talking for a few moments, then the man headed back off to the compound and Isabella viewed through the chink as the woman watched him go.

Only when she was sure he had gone, did she return and cautiously approach Isabella's hiding place and crouch down beside her.

"You should not be here," she murmured. "It is not safe for you, if they find you, they will kill you."

"I know," Isabella replied. "Come nightfall I will be gone, but I wouldn't have stood a chance out there in daylight."

"No, maybe not," the woman agreed. She hesitated, then gave Isabella a shy smile.

"I am glad you managed to get away."

"Do you know what's happened to Nick? Did they believe his story that I overpowered him?"

Isabella couldn't keep the concern from her voice and the woman looked sad.

"So, it *was* Nick who shot Badih?"

"Yes, but he had no choice."

"Badih was a bad man, a very bad man." A memory flickered over the woman's face. "I am glad he is dead, but they did not believe Nick when he said you had done it."

"What will happen to him?" Isabella asked.

"He is to be beheaded at dusk. It will be a warning to all those who think to betray my father."

"Your father? Then your father is..."

"The Preacher, yes."

"Oh." Isabella took a moment to assimilate this, then looked at the woman in pity. "What is your name?" she asked.

"Kashm," the woman replied.

"Kashm, do you know who your father is? What he does?"

The woman looked down for a long moment, then raised shamed eyes to Isabella.

"Yes," she whispered. "I know."

"Then you know how much misery and death he causes?" The woman nodded, her eyes glittering in the dim light of the shelter.

"Yes, I know."

"I can't believe that is who you are, Kashm. You are a good person, a kind person. Are you happy, knowing what he does?"

"No, but what can I do?" Kashm cried. "My mother died, and there was only my father. I had to come with him, like a dutiful daughter. But I hate it here, those men. Badih … he …"

"Kashm, did he rape you?" Isabella didn't try to sugar-coat the words, although her voice was gentle.

Kashm shook her head, the tears now slipping freely down her cheeks at the memory.

"No, but he tried, and it was only because the American, Nick, he stopped him. But always I feel Badih's eyes on me, and I know even though my father would kill him for it if the chance came – that would not be enough to stop him."

"Nick saved you?" Isabella asked, and Kashm nodded again.

"So, please, Kashm, help me to save him."

"I cannot!"

Terror filled the young Afghan girl's eyes, and she moved away from Isabella, wiping furiously at them.

"I dare not." She pleaded with Isabella to understand. "If my father found out, even though I am his daughter, he would still punish me."

"Kashm." Isabella took the trembling hand of the younger girl in her own. "Please, you must help me. Nick saved you from Badih, he saved me from being killed and now he's going to be beheaded for it."

"I can do nothing for him, or you," Kashm sobbed. "I am just a woman, what can I do?"

"Oh, Kashm." Isabella grinned fiercely in the gloom. "Never think because you are a woman that means you are weak. Now listen, this is what I need you to do."

~Chapter Eleven~
"Wait for the signal,"

After they had beaten him into submission, they'd dragged his sorry ass to a cell – the one recently inhabited by Isabella – and thrown him roughly to the floor.

Jeering at the fate that awaited him, his escort clanged shut the cell door. Nick heard the sadistic laughter of the men as they settled at a table a few paces away and left him to make his peace with God, or whatever deity his heathen American soul worshipped.

Heaving himself to a sitting position, Nick examined his injuries. Damn, probably a broken rib or two, and he'd been left with more cuts and bruises than skin, but given he was going to be dead by nightfall, it was kind of a moot point.

Isabella.

Nick closed his eyes in regret and wondered if she'd made it to the goat shelter okay. Probably, he concluded. They wouldn't have missed the chance to rub her recapture in his face.

He'd told her to wait until after nightfall, and that he would come for her. Well, he'd be dead by then, so Nick hoped she'd have the sense to think about herself and not try anything stupid.

He thought about the past two weeks, about meeting her again. When ordered to establish contact with Isabella Santorini, he had examined his feelings curiously.

It was true he had never forgotten her, and that there had never been anyone else in his life he loved as much as her. After all, she was his first love, and maybe it was correct that you never quite got over the first.

Then he'd seen her, spoken with her, taken her in his arms and kissed her, made incredible love with her ... and it had been like the eleven years never happened. He fell in love with her all over again, but this time not as a callow and idealistic boy, this time he loved as a man.

Yet for all the strength of his feelings for her, they hadn't been enough to protect her from his world, and they hadn't been enough to stop him from betraying her.

Regret pierced his soul, and once again he prayed that Isabella wouldn't do anything stupid and would find her way home. To the little house that for the day and a night he spent there with her, felt like home to him as well.

There was movement outside the bars, and he looked up to see The Preacher's young daughter, Kashm, standing there with a tray of food.

"The Preacher's orders," she said to the men. "A last meal for the condemned man."

They snorted in derision, but one of them rose and unlocked the cell door to allow her entry. Carefully, she carried the tray over to Nick, patiently waiting as he painfully pulled himself up onto the cot and held out grateful hands to take it from her. But she clutched onto it until Nick raised puzzled eyes to her soft brown ones.

"Kashm?" he murmured. She was a good kid, a nice girl who didn't deserve to be The

Preacher's daughter, and she certainly didn't deserve the way these men looked at her, and the thoughts they had about her. Thoughts they wouldn't hesitate to act on if her father were ever not there.

"I am sorry," she whispered in English, then stared fixedly at one of the dumplings on the plate. "Wait for the signal," she breathed, then thrust the tray at him and fled back to the door.

Casting a glance over her shoulder, she waited until the guard unlocked it and let her out before fleeing swiftly down the passageway and the guard sat down with his friend.

Nick pulled back into the deepening gloom of the cell. With the only light coming from the barred opening far above his head, as the sun set, long shadows were forming in the corners.

Softly, he tore the dumpling apart and pulled at the meat and vegetable contents until his fingers touched something smooth and rounded.

Glancing at the disinterested guards who were now sharing a jug of something, he swiftly slid his hand to his side and wiped the thing on the thin blanket on the cot. It was Isabella's locket.

He slipped it into his pocket, then turned his attention to the food on his plate. It looked like Isabella was planning something stupid after all, so he better build up his strength ready.

Nightfall came all too quickly, and Nick was dragged roughly from his cell and taken back to the large cavern, to be cast down on his knees before The Preacher.

"Nick, Nick, it grieves my heart that you have betrayed me." The Preacher's voice oozed with fake sincerity as he paced down from the dais and looked down at the dark head of the American man he had trusted and regarded almost fondly.

"I didn't." Even though he knew it was useless, still Nick had one last attempt to lie his way out.

"I didn't betray you. I told you, she took me by surprise and got my gun. I'm sorry about Badih, but it all happened so fast I couldn't stop her."

"Badih was an animal." The Preacher dismissed the man's death with a wave of his hand. "But he wasn't stupid, and I do not believe this weak English woman was able to do what you claim she did. So, I am giving you one last chance to change your story. Who knows, maybe I will let you live."

"I told you." Defiantly, Nick rose to his feet and stared the other man down. "She got the jump on me, grabbed my gun and shot Badih, then took off into the desert. I have no idea where she is now, probably halfway back to Kandahar if she's got any sense."

The Preacher considered his words, then shook his head in dismissal, gesturing to the guards who grabbed Nick and forced him back to his knees.

A figure loomed from the shadows. Tall and menacing, he raised his pulwar – the traditional Afghan sword – over his head, and Nick swallowed in fear.

This was it. Whatever Isabella had planned, she was too late. Frantically, he hoped that she realised this and got away while she still could.

The figure raised the pulwar and Nick stared death in the eyes, regret searing his soul at so much left undone, so much still to experience...

A loud crack echoed through the chamber. The executioner collapsed onto the stone floor with a neat hole in his temple, and all the lights went out.

Wait for the signal, Kashm said. Well, Nick figured someone shooting his would-be executioner stone dead in front of him to be a blatant signal and was already on the move when the lights went out.

The shot that killed his executor was such a display of expert marksmanship, that, if Nick had time to stop and wonder at it, he would have done. But time was the one thing he didn't have, so instead, he rolled to the left and was on his feet and moving, before any of the others in the cavern had the chance to react to the blackness in which they now found themselves.

In the dark, he cannoned heavily into someone who clutched at him, yelling hoarsely in his native language as Nick felt for his throat and chopped him to the ground, scooping up the fallen man's gun and trying desperately to figure out which way was left.

The shot came from the left, so Nick figured that was where he needed to go, but in almost total darkness it was hard to get a grip of exactly where the left was. Another shape loomed up out of the gloom and without stopping, Nick clubbed him down with the gun.

Then his outstretched hand felt the roughness of the wall and he hurried along it until the wall gave way to space and he knew he'd reached the passageway.

Falling into the gloom beyond, he reacted instinctively when someone grabbed his arm, and he twisted to tackle them.

"Nick," the figure grunted, and he realised it was Isabella. "Come on," she hissed and switched a small torch on. Although it's feeble beam barely illuminated their way, Isabella confidently led him down the long passageway until they reached the door of the kitchen.

Pausing, Isabella tapped once on it, then again. It flew open and a scared looking Kashm thrust a bulging knapsack at Isabella.

"Come with us," Isabella begged, and Nick got the sense this wasn't the first time the plea had been issued.

"I cannot." The girl shook her head, her look of terror increasing as the angry shouts echoed down the passageway. "You must go," she urged.

"Thank you, Kashm." Isabella drew the girl to her in a quick hug.

"Thank you." Nick echoed Isabella's sentiment, and Kashm flashed him a shy smile.

"You must go," she said again and pressed a key into Isabella's hand. "Lock me in," she ordered. "Then my father will believe I had nothing to do with this."

Isabella nodded and Kashm disappeared back into the gloom. Pulling the door shut, Isabella locked it. Leaving the key in the door, she pulled Nick after her down the passageway to finally emerge into a clear, starlit night.

"Come on," she ordered and gestured to where a jeep was waiting.

"That's no good," Nick told her. "They have much faster vehicles – they'll soon catch up with us."

"Not with slashed tyres, they won't," Isabella informed him with a grim smile and Nick gave a low laugh at her resourcefulness.

"Let me drive," he said. "I know the road better than you do."

Isabella jumped into the passenger seat and Nick started the engine, grinding the ancient gears as they roared away down the road, his heart still racing at their escape and how close to death he had come.

He glanced at Isabella. Bracing herself as the jeep bounced over the uneven road, she looked sideways at him. He had thought he would never see her again. In the cell, facing death, he had imagined all the things he would say to her given the chance. But now she was here, with him, he was rendered speechless.

"How did you get Kashm involved?" was all he could think to say.

"She found me hiding in the goat shed, but she didn't give me away, so I knew she was sympathetic, and I persuaded her to help."

Isabella paused and looked steadily at Nick, the moonlight making her dark eyes glitter.

"She told me you stopped Badih from raping her, so I guess she figured she owed you one."

"She's a good kid," Nick replied. "I only hope she doesn't get into trouble for helping us."

"When they find her locked in the kitchen, I think they will believe her story. Men like that, well, they tend to dismiss women as being weak and useless."

"A big mistake," Nick smiled.

"A huge mistake," Isabella agreed.

"You shot the guy with the sword...."

"I had to, he was about to deprive you of your head," Isabella interrupted wryly.

"I know, trust me, I am very grateful you did. But that shot, Isabella, that was incredible. Not many could have done it, certainly not someone without the proper training."

"What can I say?" Isabella shrugged casually. "I guess I just got lucky."

He thought she was lying, yet was unsure, because if she was, then it appeared that shooting was not the only thing she was proficient at.

~Chapter Twelve~
"What the hell happened to you, Nick?"

An hour later, they approached Kandahar and Nick drew the jeep to a halt to consider their plans.

"We're going to stick out like sore thumbs," he said. "Westerners are not exactly common in this city, certainly not Western women."

"I know," Isabella agreed, "and that is why I had Kashm pack us a few supplies."

She squirmed around in her seat, grabbed the knapsack from where she had stowed it, and began pulling items of clothing from it.

Nick softly exclaimed in surprised admiration as she threw him a set of native robes and pulled the long, all-concealing clothing of an Afghan woman out for herself.

"Clever girl," he muttered, and Isabella stopped and shot him a serious look.

"I am," she replied. "A very clever girl and I know when things are not right, and I know when I'm not being told the whole story. I'm prepared to leave it for now, until we're somewhere safe, but then – you and I – we need to talk."

"Yes," he agreed, but even then, wondered if he lied because there were some things that probably shouldn't be shared, even after all they had been through.

Hastily donning the disguise, Nick hoped they would be enough to fool a casual glance, although knew he'd have to keep his head down. Isabella with her tanned complexion and dark eyes would blend in more easily, and besides, as a woman would be overlooked and ignored.

His hazel eyes and pale skin would mark him out immediately as a Westerner. The Preacher had many contacts in the city. Nick knew word would already have been sent to be on the lookout for them, and that reaching a place of safety would be difficult, if not impossible.

But he said nothing of this to Isabella, no need to worry her until he had to, and he didn't want her to panic. Although, thinking about the way she had coped so far, Nick didn't think panicking was something Isabella Santorini did very often.

As they approached the city, they joined a tailback of other vehicles queuing to enter on the main road.

"What's going on?" Isabella asked as Nick slowed to a stop at the end of the line.

"Roadblock," he replied, and they exchanged glances before Nick put the jeep in reverse and turned them around to drive back the way they had come.

"Plan?" Isabella asked.

"We'll skirt the city, find somewhere to dump the jeep, then try to slip in on foot. I know The Preacher has eyes and ears everywhere, even has the police in his pocket – hence the roadblock – he must have contacted some of his bought cops and got them to set it up."

"So, where do we go?" Isabella asked. "Do we try to make it to the embassy? Although, which one? British or American?"

"I have contacts of my own," Nick reassured her. "I know a safe house where we can rest and decide what to do."

"I bet you do," Isabella muttered under her breath, yet when Nick looked at her in sharp enquiry, she merely shrugged and looked away.

They abandoned the jeep thirty minutes later, slipping quietly through the sleeping tents of a poorer outlying section of the city. Keeping their heads averted from the few people they encountered, Nick began to hope they would reach the safehouse undetected.

He slid a sideways glance at Isabella. Following his lead, she stole quietly through the streets, and he saw the glitter of her eyes as her head twisted to scan their surroundings.

She was good at this, he thought, too good for your average citizen, no matter how clever she claimed to be. The single shot to a moving target from a distance that had downed a man – through a crowd of other men all pressing forward in sick anticipation of a bloodletting – that had been more than mere luck.

Her ingenuity and resourcefulness in executing his rescue and their escape were the actions of a cool head and cried of years of intensive training. For the first time, Nick wondered if what he had been told about Isabella Santorini was correct.

He drew to a halt, an expletive soft on his breath. Ahead of them, on the street they needed to take, was a checkpoint. Peering around the corner he hurriedly flattened himself to the wall, glancing at Isabella in concern.

"Checkpoint," he muttered at her raised brow.

She squirmed past him and looked for herself, before putting her lips very close to his ear.

"There's only four of them."

"Maybe, but they have guns and there's no cover, so they'll see us coming."

"Watch and learn," Isabella said, and before he could stop her, she had picked up a large carrying basket laying abandoned against the wall and hefted it up onto her shoulder the way Afghan women carried piles of laundry or food.

"Isabella, no..." he hissed, but it was too late, she had stepped out into the street and was slowly approaching the checkpoint.

In agony, he watched her approach the police, her whole demeanour one of a humble woman going about her business – although what an honest woman was doing out on the streets this time of night – was something Nick hoped the men didn't stop to think of.

Isabella had reached the men now, and one of them called out to her to stop and state her business. Nick knew Isabella spoke no Afghan and prayed by the note of enquiry in the man's voice it was obvious to her what he meant.

Isabella paused and with signs of relief put the basket down on the ground as if it weighed substantially more than it did.

Casually, their guns held loosely – after all, she was a woman, so what threat could she possibly pose – two of the men sauntered over and lifted the lid on the empty basket.

Isabella had been waiting for that moment.

As it registered with the men that something was amiss, she struck. A hand like iron chopped at the throat of one as a firm kick shattered the kneecap of the other and both hit the ground.

Whirling in mid-air, Isabella flew at the other men who were slow to react – too slow – barely having time to bring their guns up before she was upon them and smashed their heads together so violently it knocked them both cold.

Then, for good measure, she twisted back and knocked the man lying on the ground clutching his knee out cold, before he could even think of doing anything stupid like shooting her.

By the time a stunned Nick had sprinted down the street to join her, she had dragged one of the men into an adjoining alley and hidden him in the deep shadows there.

"Isabella…" he began.

"Help me," she hissed. "Before anyone else comes along." Silently, he did as she ordered, his admiration of her swelling in his chest until he could barely breathe but realising, with a sinking sense of disappointment, that this was yet further proof of her true identity.

"Where to?" Isabella asked, and he nodded along the now clear street.

"Not far, another ten minutes or so – that's if we don't run into any more trouble."

"We'll be ready for it if we do," Isabella assured him, her mouth twisted into a grimace, and Nick got the feeling she was enjoying herself.

The safehouse was located behind a shop selling fish, and their noses wrinkled at the pungent odour as Nick led them confidently down an alley beside the shop, and over a wall to drop down into a small courtyard where piles of refuse muffled the sound of their feet.

Nick gestured to a nondescript wooden door in a corner of the courtyard and Isabella nodded, pulled the gun from beneath her robes and kept back as Nick softly tapped on the door, waited a few moments, then tapped again. Long minutes passed before the door creaked open and a figure could be seen in the gloom of the interior.

Nick murmured soft words in Afghan, and the figure stepped back to allow them entry. Isabella followed Nick in, glancing curiously at the shadowy man who grinned at her, his white teeth glinting in the dark.

Nick turned to the man and pressed something into his hand, and more speedy conversation flew between them. Not for the first time over the last few days, Isabella wished Afghan were one of the five languages she spoke, especially when the man slipped past her out into the night, closing the door as he left.

"Who was that?" she asked, following Nick up twisty stairs into a small room at the top, dimly lit by a lantern perched on a rickety table. A bed sat in one corner, and a chipped and stained sink stood in the other.

"That was a friend," Nick replied. "He's taking a message to another friend of mine – one who can get us out of here."

"What friend?"

"Isabella, please." Nick dumped the backpack on the bed. "You just have to trust me."

Isabella nodded slowly, looking around the room, noticing a semi-open door beyond which a basic toilet could be spotted.

"I too have friends," she said. "Maybe your *friend* could take a message to them as well."

"Maybe," he agreed, his eyes narrowing in suspicion. "Isabella..." he began.

"Nick?" she replied.

Tension seethed in the air between them as mistrust and doubt finally bubbled to the surface, and all the secrets and deceptions of the past week erupted.

And suddenly, two weapons were being pointed at two hearts which beat with the painful certainty that they had been betrayed.

Harsh, ragged gasps echoed in the small room as Nick stared into the barrel of Isabella's weapon, and she stared into his. A moment of confrontation – Nick knew it had long been on the table – but he hadn't expected it to go down like this.

He never thought that when the moment of truth was finally upon him, he would be holding a gun on the woman he loved. And he had never imagined that she would be holding one on him.

"I know what you are," Isabella ground out, her voice clipped and precise. "I know exactly what you are."

"Oh yeah," Nick drawled. "And what do you think I am then?"

"Bad," she spat in disgust. "A drug runner, a lackey for the likes of The Preacher. What the hell happened to you, Nick? The boy I knew would never have sunk to such levels."

"Is that what you think?" he demanded, surprised that it hurt although really, what else did he expect from her?

"Do you really believe that of me?" he continued. "The man is not so very different from the boy, Isabella."

"Then explain yourself," she demanded. "Explain what you're doing here, in the pay of The Preacher. You knew exactly who and what he was, so don't try and plead innocence. You're guilty as hell. I'd be doing the world a favour if I put a bullet between your eyes."

"So, do it then," he said, and slowly lowered his hand and dropped the gun onto the bed behind him.

"Do it." He took a step toward her.

"Stay where you are," she snarled. "Because I will do it, so help me god, Nick, I will drop you where you stand."

"If you don't trust me, Isabella, then do it, shoot me. Because when I told you to trust me, I was telling the truth. You *can* trust me."

"Yeah, right," Isabella drawled sarcastically. "Trust you? How can I? You've done nothing but lie to me since walking back into my life?"

"Yes," he agreed, taking another step forward. "I have been lying to you, almost every word I've said to you has been a lie – except when I told you to trust me, and when I said I loved you – that was the truth."

He was directly in front of her now and took the barrel of her gun and pressed it to his forehead. Feeling the cold of the metal on his flesh, his eyes met hers in total candour.

~Chapter Thirteen~
"They're breaking the door down,"

For a moment, he was horribly afraid Isabella was going to take him at his word and shoot him, but then her hand began to shake and with a growl of frustration, she pulled the gun away and stepped back.

"So, what the hell is the truth then, Nick," she demanded. "What are you?"

"I'm CIA," he said.

"CIA?"

"Yes," he replied, and she believed him.

"Okay." She took a deep breath to steady herself, then tucked the gun into her robe. "So, you're with The Preacher because…"

"I'm deep undercover."

"That makes sense, I guess, but you could have told me." Nick raised a brow at her, and Isabella threw up her hands in resignation. "No, I suppose you couldn't have."

"So, now I've spilt the beans, it's your turn."

"What do you mean?"

"Why don't you tell me the truth about who Isabella Santorini is, and why she is a 'person of interest' to the CIA? A person of such interest, that when they discovered our past connection, they ordered me to make contact with you even though I was already deep undercover on another vital mission."

"So, our meeting was no coincidence then?" Isabella asked, heart clenching at the thought.

"No, they've been watching you for a while now. You always seem to pop up in places you are not supposed to be, Isabella. It raised certain *concerns* about you. As I knew you, and because I was already in London, I was ordered to let you see me on the street."

"What about if I hadn't followed you that day?" Isabella asked, and Nick shrugged.

"There were contingency plans in place for me to accidentally run into you again."

"I see." Isabella considered his words and the implications for her. "What do you think I am?"

"I'm not sure. I'm positive you're not doing anything shady. The girl I knew back then wouldn't, and I'm damn sure the woman I know now wouldn't either."

"Thanks for that, I suppose," Isabella said.

"I take it you're British Intelligence of some sort. MI5, or MI6, or something..."

"Else...?"

Nick's eyes narrowed in contemplation. "There are rumours," he began. "Of an organisation with no affiliation to any single country, but I thought they were just that ... rumours..."

Isabella stared at him but remained silent.

"Right," he said and rubbed a hand over a jaw that still throbbed from her blow. "That explains ... a lot..."

"I was ordered to exploit my relationship with you," Isabella told him. "The DEA knew you were involved with The Preacher – there are pictures of you in Boston with known associates of his –

but couldn't get close enough to prove anything. It was believed I could."

"The DEA?" Nick's surprise was evident. "Were they working this case as well?"

"Yes," Isabella smiled wryly. "I don't suppose it would be at all possible for your various law enforcement agencies to actually talk to one another occasionally."

"Loose talk costs lives," Nick told her, and Isabella nodded.

"It does indeed."

"So, when you went to bed with me, it was because of the mission?"

"Yes," she replied honestly and saw him wince. "As it was for you, but I still wanted to. Even though I knew what they believed about you, what I thought you had become, I couldn't help myself. I wanted you, Nick."

"Isabella," he breathed, and somehow, they were in each other's arms. "I love you," he said, and she nodded.

"I know."

"The Empire Strikes Back," he murmured.

"The only Star Wars film worth bothering with," she replied, as his lips moved over hers. She felt them curve into an amused grin, then he was kissing her and nothing else mattered.

Exhaustion claimed them soon after and they both fell into the sleep of total fatigue as the sun crept through the blinds at the window.

Opening his eyes an hour later, Nick tightened his grip around Isabella as she lay sleeping by his side with her head on his chest.

His relief that they were effectively on the same side was immense. Although he knew their future relationship would be – complicated – to say the least, it was doable.

He wondered what time it was, just past dawn by the looks of it, and a sense of unease crept into his mind. Azim should have been back by now. He should have been back an hour ago.

Maybe he had come back and was waiting downstairs, not wanting to disturb them. But that explanation didn't sit right, and Nick gently untangled his arm from under Isabella, not wanting to wake her unnecessarily, and eased himself from the bed.

Swiftly pulling on his clothes, he crept down the stairs and peered into the still shut and empty shop. Undoing the catch on the back door, he stuck his head out into the courtyard and felt the stillness of the early morning settle onto him.

Closing and locking the door again behind him, he hurried back up the stairs to the small room where Isabella was stirring in the bed.

"What is it?" she asked, and he placed a finger to his lips, oozing along the wall to look through the corner of the blind out onto the apparently deserted street below.

"Get dressed," he told her. "I think we're about to have company."

Without another word, Isabella hurried to comply, snatching up her gun from the table and tucking it into her jacket, before pulling the all-encompassing robe over her head.

"Not that way," said Nick as she crossed to the staircase. "Up here." He indicated a hatchway in the ceiling and lifted the rickety table to stand beneath it. Scrambling up onto it, he pushed the hatchway open and pulled himself up and through the narrow opening out onto the flat roof. Keeping low, he squirmed around and reached a hand back down to Isabella. But she was already pulling herself up and through to lie on the roof beside him.

"They're breaking the door down," she hissed, and he nodded, quickly closing the hatchway after her.

"Follow me," he ordered, "and keep low."

Using his elbows, he wiggled to the edge of the building, keeping below the parapet, aware there were probably still men on the street below looking for them. He reached the edge and waited for Isabella to crawl up beside him.

"We need to hang over the edge and drop," he told her, and she nodded her understanding, copying as he crawled up and over the parapet to hang by his hands facing the wall of the building.

Hand over hand, he moved along the building, with Isabella following him. The thought flashed through his mind how strong she was, to be able to support her entire weight with her arms, then he was at the corner of the building and easing around it to drop down into the alleyway below.

There was a soft thud as Isabella landed beside him and flashed him a quick, inquiring glance. Wordlessly, he gestured down the alley and she nodded.

Together they moved silently to the end of the alleyway and peered around. Two men, weapons tightly clasped as they watched the shop front – clearly expecting their targets to come from there. Nick and Isabella exchanged glances, then moved as one entity. There were a couple of grunts, and the two unconscious men were dragged back into the alley and left in a doorway.

Quickly scanning the empty street, they heard loud voices and the sound of furniture being smashed inside the shop, and Nick assumed their would-be assailants were expressing their anger at their escape.

He gestured towards the alleyway on the opposite side of the street, then hurried towards it with Isabella close on his heels. Reaching the relative safety of the gloomy enclosed space, he paused to consider their next move.

"What now?" Isabella breathed in his ear.

"Assuming Azim never made it to my friend, we need to try and reach him ourselves."

"Can we?"

"Maybe," he shrugged. "Anyway, we have to try because we don't have many other options."

Isabella apparently agreed because she remained silent, merely following him as he set off down the alleyway, trying to get his bearings. Thankfully, it was still so early not many were out on the streets to notice them.

Less than an hour later, they knocked on a stout, wooden door. Keeping their heads down and trying not to draw attention to themselves, they waited for long minutes until a small hatch opened in the wood and a face peered through the ornate grill covering the opening.

A voice asked something in enquiry, and Nick replied in another language Isabella was unfamiliar with. The hatch slammed shut and even longer minutes passed before the door suddenly opened and a figure beckoned them in.

Blinking in the gloom after the glare of the street, Isabella looked around at the interior of the dwelling, reminiscent of those she had visited in Marrakech. Ahead, she could see the brightness of an interior courtyard, beautifully decorated with a colourful mosaic floor. A charming fountain played at its heart and lush foliage beckoned them in alluringly.

"Nick Eastman," said a voice, and Isabella turned to see a man in long flowing robes approaching Nick with his hands outstretched and a welcoming smile on his face.

"Karim," Nick said.

The man took his hands and looked closely at him, the smile slipping from his face as he took in Nick's bedraggled appearance.

"But what is wrong, my friend?" Karim asked in concern.

"Karim, did Azim deliver my message?"

"Azim? No, it has been many moons since I last saw our mutual friend. Why?"

"I think something may have happened to him," replied Nick, his face pulling into lines of concern.

"I will make enquiries," Karim said and waved a hand at the pair of silent giants who followed him. Wordlessly, one melted away into the shadows and Karim looked at Isabella curiously.

"Karim, this is my ... friend ... Isabella Santorini. Isabella, this is my long-time friend and ally, Karim Idrissi."

"Enchanted to meet you," Karim said, and took her hand, bowing low over it in greeting.

"Thank you," murmured Isabella. "Thank you for inviting us into your beautiful home."

"Ah," exclaimed Karim with pleasure. "Beauty and charm, a lethal combination for any man to resist." He glanced knowingly at Nick. "Your pleasure in my home pleases me, my dear, and I bid you stay as long as you need."

"Thank you," said Isabella again. "Although, I am curious. The layout is more Moroccan than I expected."

"Intelligence as well as beauty and charm," Karim gushed. "I can see why the lovely Isabella is your ... friend."

"Karim is Moroccan," Nick explained. "But he upset certain *parties* there and had to leave in rather a hurry. Relocating to Kandahar, he decided to recreate his home here down to the last detail."

"Within these walls, I can at least pretend I have never left my beloved country," Karim said. "But come, where are my manners? I see you need assistance. I will order baths and clean clothing to be provided."

"It would be best if no one learns that we are here," Nick began, and Karim silenced him with a lifted hand.

"My staff are the epitome of loyalty and discretion. None shall know of your presence."

"Thank you, Karim," said Nick, and Isabella nodded gratefully.

"Please follow Omar." Karim waved towards the second of his giant bodyguards. "He will show you to your rooms ... separate rooms," he said. "For the sake of respectability."

"Of course," agreed Nick blandly.

"Oh, and Nick," Karim said as they turned to follow the bulk of Omar. "Please, I would be most grateful if you could take a good long bath."

~Chapter Fourteen~
"I just want to go home."

Grinning, Nick nodded, and Isabella's nose wrinkled in shamed acknowledgement that they both smelled a little ripe and she should probably have a good long bath as well.

The room Isabella was shown to felt cool and shady, with a balcony looking out over the lush courtyard below. A few moments after Omar and Nick left, there was a shy knock at the door.

Opening it, Isabella found a young girl with an armful of clothing and downcast eyes that only briefly met Isabella's, before she placed the clothing on the bed and scuttled into the adjoining room to run Isabella a bath.

Unused to being waited on, Isabella attempted to engage the girl in conversation but soon realised it was futile. Either the girl didn't speak English or didn't wish to speak to her, and Isabella lapsed into silence, watching as the girl ran a deep bath in the beautiful mosaic-tiled pool, took luxuriously fluffy towels from a cupboard and laid them beside it.

The girl crossed to Isabella and attempted to start unbuttoning her shirt, but Isabella pulled her hands away and ushered her to the door.

"It's fine," she said, shaking her head and smiling. "I can undress myself, honestly."

The girl lightly touched her shirt again and then pointed to herself.

"You want my clothes?" Isabella guessed. "Okay, wait one moment."

Going into the bathroom she found a robe hanging behind the door and quickly changed into it, bringing her clothes out in a neat pile, and handing them to the servant, who bobbed her head thankfully and then left.

Isabella shut the door, then leaned back on its ornately carved surface and took a long, deep breath. So much had happened over the past few days, she needed a moment to reflect and assess.

Isabella wondered what was happening back home. By now her disappearance would have been discovered, and she knew Sebastian would leave no stone unturned trying to find her.

Wondering if Karim possessed a phone or had internet capabilities, Isabella determined to ask to use one or the other to contact her cousin and let him know of her whereabouts.

Although Isabella trusted Nick now, she did not know Karim and was reluctant to place her safety solely in a stranger's hands. No, the sooner she contacted Sebastian and arrangements were made to get them home – or at least to a more secure location – the happier Isabella would be.

Fingers tapped softly on the door, and she pulled it open, startling Nick who was raising his hand to knock again. Under one arm he held a pile of clean clothing and his eyes met hers with the light of mischief dancing in them.

"Can I come in?" he asked.

Isabella leant on the doorframe and quirked her brow at him. "I'm not sure. I don't think Karim would find that very respectable."

"Karim knows full well how things stand, he just doesn't want to shock his staff."

"Hmm." Isabella pretended to consider it, then relented and pulled him inside, closing the door and locking it against any unwanted intrusions.

"This Karim," she asked seriously, pushing Nick's hands away as he tried to pull her to him. "Who is he? What's his story?"

"He was a prominent businessman in Morocco but when he refused to play ball with some corrupt officials who wanted to use his business as a front for gun-running, he had to vacate the country rather quickly."

"I see, but how did you meet him?"

"Through a mutual contact. Karim has helped the CIA before with delicate missions in Afghanistan. I think he views it as his small way of fighting the corruption that is rife in this part of the world."

"Do you trust him?"

"Implicitly. He's one of the guys in white hats, Isabella. Honestly, I'd trust Karim with my life."

"Well, that's what you are doing," she replied. "And you are trusting him with mine. I'm not sure about this, Nick. After all that has happened, I don't think it's wise to trust anyone."

"You, my darling, are too suspicious." Nick tapped a kiss on her nose. "Even if you don't trust him, trust me. Now, it would be a shame to let that hot bath go cold, and I didn't want to say anything before, but you do kind of stink."

"You're not exactly a bundle of sweet peas yourself," Isabella retorted, allowing herself to be propelled into the bathroom where the scented warm water was seducing her with its promise of scrubbing away the sweat and grime of several days without a shower.

"I'll scrub your back if you scrub mine." Nick leered suggestively at her, and Isabella laughed.

"Deal," she murmured, as his hands began to undress her, and this time Isabella didn't object.

Awaking later, Isabella guessed from the lengthening shadows that it was late afternoon, so slipped out from under Nick's arm and went to see if there was such a thing as a toothbrush and a hairbrush in the luxurious bathroom.

Dressing for a much-anticipated dinner with their host, Isabella struggled into the traditional Moroccan woman's attire the servant had left, feeling like a harem girl from the Arabian Nights book she had read as a youngster.

Lying on the bed already dressed and looking like a Western version of The Sheik, Nick raised his eyebrows at her difficulty arranging the long scarf that came with the outfit.

"I think that double crosses over the throat and then hangs down the back," he helpfully suggested and laughed at her expression.

"You look beautiful," he said when she'd finished fiddling and looked at the result in the ornate mirror standing in the corner of the room.

"I prefer my clothes," Isabella grunted.

"You'll get them back," Nick assured her, and Isabella nodded, then clutched at her stomach as it emitted a huge rumble.

"Come on," Nick laughed, clambering off her bed and holding out an arm. "Let's get you fed, and we can discuss with Karim what to do next."

"Go home," muttered Isabella, angrily fighting down an overwhelming urge to cry. "I just want to go home."

"We will," Nick promised and pulled her to him for a warm and comforting hug. "Don't worry, we're safe, everything will be all right now."

Dinner was delicious, a sumptuous feast placed on a low table as they sat cross-legged on deep cushions. Trying to remember her table manners and not tear into the food like a feral animal, Isabella half-listened to the conversation between the two men as they discussed people she didn't know and events she'd never heard of.

"Is there news of Azim?" Isabella's ears pricked up at Nick's question, and she stopped eating to fix her gaze upon their host's face as his expression changed to one of deep regret.

"I am truly sorry, my friend, but my sources inform me Azim was found dead this morning."

"How?" Nick's jaw tightened in angry concern.

"He was found in the marketplace with his throat cut. It looks like your enemies found him before he could reach me."

Regretfully, Nick nodded, his eyes thoughtful at the implications. "Karim, I don't think we were followed here, but we need to leave. We can't risk bringing danger into your home."

"Do not worry." Karim waved away his concern. "They will not dare to come here. You are safe within these walls, but after we have eaten you must contact the authorities to arrange transportation out of Afghanistan as quickly as possible. I think to stay any longer would be dangerous for your health, and I would hate for anything to happen to you, my friend."

"Yes, I need to report in, and get Isabella safely home." Nick agreed. "The Preacher kidnapped her believing he could use her against me."

"That man is an animal," Karim retorted, his face twisting into a moue of distaste. "His methods are crude and heavy-handed, like breaking into an almond with a sledgehammer."

"That may be so," Nick agreed. "But he's also a very dangerous man and with the number of people in authority that he has in his pocket, the sooner we get out of the country, the better."

The meal concluded, servants silently moved in to clear the table and lay out platters of dried fruits and nuts, and tiny cups of thick coffee – which Nick accepted, but Isabella declined.

A servant murmured in Karim's ear, and he smiled at Isabella warmly. "Charming though you are in my country's native dress, I am sensing you are finding it a little uncomfortable."

Isabella squirmed with mortification that he had noticed her constant repositioning of the scarf and her fiddling with the low-cut top that revealed more than she was comfortable with.

"My servant has informed me that your clothes are now dry if you wish to change back."

"Thank you," murmured Isabella.

"She will escort you back to your room where you will find they have been placed."

"There's no need, I'm sure I can find the way."

"I insist, my dear. It is a large house, and it would be all too easy for you to take a wrong turn and lose your way. She will wait while you change and then escort you back."

"Actually," Isabella decided, as a wave of exhaustion threatened to drown her. "I'm really tired, so I think I'm going to call it a night."

"Of course." Karim rose courteously and bowed gracefully over her hand. "It was truly an honour to meet you. I look forward to renewing our acquaintance over breakfast. Goodnight.

"Goodnight," said Isabella.

Nick too rose and gently touched her hand.

"You okay on your own?"

"I'm fine."

"Want me to tap on the door before I turn in?"

"No," was what her mouth said. "I'll probably be asleep." *Yes*, were what her eyes said. *After all that has happened today, I want to be with you.*

"Okay, goodnight," was all he said, but his smile let her know he understood her message.

Following the servant up hidden stairs and along twisting corridors, Isabella realised without the girl's guidance she would have lost her way. She hoped Nick would have no trouble finding his way back when he'd finished having coffee with Karim.

"Thank you," she said when they arrived back at her room. The servant gave her a smile and disappeared into the gloom of the passageway.

Isabella entered the room, pleased to see her clothes lying on the bed. Servants had been in whilst they had been at dinner because the bed was freshly made, the bathroom cleaned, and new towels lay ready to use.

Lamps had been lit so the room appeared cosy and inviting, and Isabella stifled a yawn. Despite having slept almost the whole day away, she still felt tired and eyed the bed longingly.

Damn, she'd forgotten to ask Karim about using the phone to contact Sebastian. Isabella hesitated, wondering whether to leave it to the morning. No, it was too important to leave any longer. Sebastian would be frantic with worry, and her family would be beginning to wonder where she was as well.

Sighing, Isabella changed and slipped from her room. Faced with the endless gloomy passageway she thought about waiting until Nick came up, but there was no telling how long he would be with Karim. Isabella decided she couldn't wait and stole down the corridor.

Moving quietly, Isabella crept down a twisting flight of stairs only to be confronted with a choice of which way to go at the bottom. Had it been right or left to get back to the dining room? She couldn't remember so picked a direction at random, soon realising that she had no memory of this stretch of corridor.

She hesitated, then heard voices up ahead and the clanging of pots and pans. It must be the kitchen, and Isabella decided to throw herself on the mercy of the servants and admit that she'd got lost after all.

Walking to the door standing ajar at the end, Isabella paused with her hand on the wood as a burst of male laughter erupted from within and then a strangely familiar voice said something.

Cautiously, Isabella sidled up to the crack in the door and peered through. At the long wooden table in the middle of the room, sat three men passing around a thick bottle of some sort of dark liquid. Two of them Isabella had never seen before, but the third man was Azim.

The man their host swore had been found in the marketplace with his throat cut, was sitting in his kitchen very much alive.

~Chapter Fifteen~
"I think Karim drugged your coffee."

For a split second, Isabella froze with indecision, then moved, swiftly and quietly, away from the door.

Azim lived, yet their host swore he had died, which meant...

Which meant Karim had lied to them.

Why?

And what else had he lied about?

All of Isabella's senses on red alert, she sped down the gloomy passageway until she reached the bottom of the stairs again, then carried straight on.

This time she found the dining room, but it was abandoned with no sign of either Nick or Karim.

Cautiously she approached the table and noticed the smashed coffee cup on the floor with dregs of the thick, caffeine heavy liquid lying amongst the shards.

Where was Nick?

She had to find him.

Wondering if he'd gone to her room, in the few moments she had lingered outside the kitchen door, Isabella hurried back and climbed the staircase, looking out for Karim or his heavies with every step she took.

Her initial vague feelings of distrust of the man had solidified into an absolute conviction that something was very wrong.

Nick had said to trust Karim, that he was a friend, but Isabella didn't believe that. Why had the man lied to them about Azim?

She could only think of one reason – to cover his tracks. Someone had known how to find them at the safehouse. The only person who knew they were there was Azim.

And as Azim – far from being dead – was currently drinking in Karim's kitchen, he must have told their host, who then sent men to catch them at the safehouse.

But they failed, and she and Nick had got away – only to deliver themselves to Karim after all – like lambs to the slaughter.

So why had Karim not taken them prisoner straight away? What motive did he have for waiting? For allowing them to sleep and bathe and eat.

Isabella couldn't think of a reason why, but only knew that she and Nick needed to get out of this house of shadows and lies as quickly as possible.

She reached the balcony overlooking the courtyard and saw a dark shadow slumped on the floor outside her room.

"Nick!"

Quickly she ran to him and began to pull him to his feet.

His eyes fluttered open, and he tried to focus on her face.

"Isabella …?" he slurred. "I don't feel too good."

"No, I think Karim drugged your coffee."

"Wah? Why … why would he do that?"

"Because he's been lying to us. Azim is very much alive and is in this house. We have to get out of here, Nick, this whole thing is a setup."

"No, Karim … wouldn't … he's my friend."

"I don't think he is anymore."

Isabella grunted as she finally managed to heave the almost dead weight of her man up and onto his feet, bracing him as he swayed.

"Isabella…"

"Come on, we need to get out of here."

"No … you have to leave me…"

"I'm not leaving you."

"You must; I'll only slow you down. You must go, get to the British embassy, tell them everything. They can contact the CIA and they'll come and get me."

Her head saw the sense of what he was saying, but her heart refused to even consider the plan.

"I'm not leaving you," she repeated and started to drag him back towards the stairs.

"Have to," he muttered again, his head lolling as the drug took a deeper hold of his system and blackness threatened to pull him under.

"Come on," Isabella snarled. "Shift your pretty boy arse and help me."

"You think my ass is pretty?"

"No, I think your *arse* is pretty, no donkeys involved."

"Wah?"

"Never mind, come on."

They were at the top of the stairs now and Isabella despaired of getting them both down and to the door before they were discovered.

"Leave me."

"Never, we go together like meatballs and spaghetti, remember?"

"Yeah," he grinned at the memory, then his head lolled forward, and he slipped from her grasp, falling to the next bend in the stairs.

Isabella winced at his groan of pain and hurried down to help him to his feet.

Reaching the bottom of the stairs, she dragged him back in the direction of the dining room.

She was pretty sure it was towards the front of the house, the street side, so logically where the front door was located.

Gritting her teeth with the strain, she shifted Nick's body until the full weight of it was across her shoulders and half carried, half dragged him with down the gloomy passageway.

Breaking into the still perfection of the courtyard, she heard the tinkling of the fountain in the evening air and saw starlight twinkling high up above them.

There!

There was the front door.

Hobbling with exertion, Isabella let Nick's weight slide to the floor beside the ornately carved wooden doors and frantically tried to see how to open them.

Bolts top and bottom, they were easily slid back, but the doors remained shut firm and she realised the key needed to open them was missing.

"Leaving so soon?"

Her heart thudding, Isabella whirled to find Karim standing behind them, surrounded by several large burly men, including Azim who flashed his teeth at her in a mocking grin.

"Let us go," she demanded.

"Oh, I think not," Karim replied.

"Why are you doing this?"

"Believe me, I truly regret the necessity, but I am in debt to a certain, very influential person who has held a grudge against Nick Eastman for five long years. By handing him over I cancel out my debt."

"Karim … no…"

Nick's eyes were heavy as he stared in drugged disbelief at his former friend.

"I am sorry, Nick." A look of regret flickered across his swarthy face.

"But there can be no friendships in business. Take him," he ordered, waving a hand at the men behind him.

"You'll have to come through me."

Isabella dropped into a fighting stance ready to tear them all into shreds if that's what it took to get her and Nick to safety.

Karim hesitated, then shrugged.

"Take her," he commanded. "But don't kill her. The Preacher wants her alive."

Isabella barely had time to react to his words before the men were upon her and she was fighting for her life.

Two of them she managed to disable immediately with savage blows to the throat which made them drop like stones.

The others gave growls of rage and attacked her like a pack of wild animals bringing down their prey.

Her mind going blank, Isabella let all her training come to the fore and simply absorbed herself into the moment.

Kick, duck, punch, and twist – the fight moved away from the door and spilt into the courtyard, and Isabella used the large ceramic pots to dodge behind.

Another heavy hit the ground as Isabella slammed his head against the rim of the fountain and he collapsed in a heap on the floor.

Azim rushed at her, but Isabella easily dealt with the slender older man, throwing him over her shoulder in a slickly perfect move that would have had her martial arts instructor from long ago applauding in approval.

Then it was just her and Omar.

Facing each other across the tiled mosaic floor now slick with the blood of his comrades, the massive mountain of a man grinned a slow nasty smirk at her, flexing his meaty hands in his eagerness to take her on.

Panting hoarsely, Isabella stared back at him, suddenly becoming aware of how much of her hurt and how exhausted she was.

"Miss Santorini."

Isabella glanced over to Karim, registering with horror the long, curved dagger held to Nick's unconscious throat.

"Suliman would prefer him alive, but I'm sure he will settle for his corpse instead."

"Don't," Isabella muttered. "Please…"

"Ah, but you are the one who holds the power of life and death over him, my dear. If you submit, then Nick remains alive – although I cannot guarantee what Suliman has in store for him."

Karim shuddered with delicate distaste.

"I do not think it will be pleasant, but at least you will not be forced to witness as I slit his throat in front of you and you watch his lifeblood spill. Knowing you could have saved him."

Isabella hesitated, and opposite her Omar shifted in anticipation.

"Come now, Miss Santorini, make your decision. What is it to be?"

He pressed the blade into the soft flesh of Nick's throat and a thin trickle of blood oozed over the brightness of the knife-edge.

Isabella gave up.

Her body slumping in despair she simply nodded, and Karim gestured towards Omar.

"Bind her. The Preacher's men will be here any moment so she must be secured ready for them.

Holding out her hands in resignation, Isabella felt the cold touch of steel as Omar clicked a pair of handcuffs on her and shoved her at Karim.

"You fight well," he breathed in her ear. "For a woman."

He laughed as Isabella struggled frantically in his grasp, intending to wipe the sadistic smirk from his face.

She wanted to go to Nick, to check he was all right, but Omar was dragging her past him, through the front doors that Karim unlocked with a large iron key and then out onto the street, where a truck awaited them.

Bodily lifted and thrown into the back of the vehicle by rough hands – Isabella's last sighting of Nick was of him lying unconscious on the floor – the wound on his throat standing out in vivid scarlet relief.

Struggling to sit, she was booted to the floor of the truck and a harsh voice growled at her in broken English to stay down.

Isabella's brain frantically raced through her options.

There weren't many, and none of them looked very promising.

As the truck crunched into gear and lurched around the corner, gathering speed down the crowded narrow street, the one thought that hammered at her mind like a persistent toothache, was the memory of Nick lying there, and the fear that she would never see him again.

~Chapter Sixteen~
"Don't play games with me,"

Deposited back into her original cell, Isabella cursed the day Karim had ever been born and spent a satisfying minute imagining what she would do to the Moroccan *businessman* when she got her hands on him.

If she ever got her hands on him, she amended and looked ruefully at the stout handcuffs that still confined her slender wrists.

Searching the cell, she felt along every inch of the rough rock walls for something – anything – that she could use to pick the lock. There was nothing.

Inspiration suddenly striking, Isabella sat down on the cot and worried at the button on her shirt until she got it open.

Then she began to painstakingly pick at the edge of her bra, ripping at the fabric with her broken fingernails until at last, she felt it give and was able to tease out the underwire.

It was gloomy in the cell, the only illumination being a single bulb swinging from the ceiling in the passageway, and the glint of moonlight coming through the bars far above her head. Isabella patiently worked at the lock of the handcuffs with the thin and pliable piece of metal, until at last there was a faint click, and Isabella grinned to herself in triumph.

Now, for the door to the cell. Unlike last time, when two guards had permanently been posted on watch, they had left her alone and Isabella briefly wondered why.

Perhaps The Preacher was undermanned, maybe his precious manpower was needed elsewhere, or maybe, once again, he had underestimated her abilities because she was a woman and therefore powerless.

Whatever the reason, Isabella thanked god for it and moved to the cell door and examined the lock. An old-fashioned tumbler lock and key mechanism, if she'd had her usual bag of tricks, she would have opened it in a heartbeat.

She didn't though. All she had was a flimsy piece of wire already showing signs of wear and tear from picking the handcuffs.

Still, it was all she had, so Isabella softly inserted it into the lock and attempted to fool the mechanism, but it was no use. The wire was too thin and pliable.

Cursing to herself, Isabella tried repeatedly, until finally the wire snapped into two pieces and fell to the ground.

Patiently, she settled down to pick out the other underwire, but loud male voices echoing down the passageway had her hastily re-buttoning her shirt and loosely pulling the handcuffs back on so they looked secure, but one yank would send them flying.

Four of them, he'd sent four men to escort her, all with weapons trained on her and expressions that promised they meant business if she didn't comply.

So, Isabella went meekly with them, biding her time, and looking for an opportunity. After all, she couldn't help Nick if she were lying dead with a bullet through her heart.

Besides, there was an edginess to the men. They were rank with the sharp smell of adrenalin and fear, and Isabella sensed from their body language that these were confused and anxious men. As such, they would be trigger happy and likely to shoot first and explain later.

Watching her footing on the uneven surface of the passageway floor, Isabella still noticed evidence of preparations for a hasty departure.

Men scurried by carrying crates and bundles of weapons and supplies. Barely bothering to glance her way, they pressed against the walls of the passageway as Isabella and her escort passed by before they hastened off on obviously vital chores.

Even in the cavern where The Preacher held court there were signs of things being packed away, and Isabella wondered if fear of their location having been compromised was behind the evacuation.

Marched to the very centre of the large space, Isabella's escort threw her roughly to her knees in front of the dais where The Preacher was waiting to receive her, his hands on his beefy hips as he coldly surveyed her.

A smirk of satisfaction played over his lips at the sight of her on her knees before him, helpless and vulnerable.

"You have caused me no small amount of trouble," he began.

"I'm *so* sorry," Isabella drawled. "And after you'd gone to so much trouble to be *such* a gracious host."

"I want to know whether Nick Eastman has divulged my location to anyone?"

"How should I know?" Isabella shrugged dismissively.

"Don't play games with me," he warned. "He is obviously working for some American law enforcement agency."

"I'm not," Isabella retorted. "If you wanted to know how much Nick has reported back to his bosses at the CIA or the FBI or Homeland Security – or whatever the hell he is – then you should have brought us both back."

"Believe me, I wanted to," The Preacher ground out with obvious frustration. "But Idrissi had other plans for him, so I had to settle for just recovering you."

"Oh, shame." Isabella pouted in sympathy. "But I understand, after all, Idrissi is a much bigger fish than you, so what could you do."

"He is not bigger than me."

The Preacher's eyes spat fire at the suggestion he was any less powerful than Karim.

"But it would have been, let's say, detrimental to my health to come between the man who wanted Nick Eastman and his revenge."

"Why?" Isabella demanded, her heart pounding in fear for Nick.

"Who wanted him? And why? What will he do to him?"

"That is none of your concern now," The Preacher informed her. "And as to what he will do to him, well, let's just say this individual's reputation is well known and even I feel pity for Eastman, despite his betrayal of me."

"You're a monster," Isabella stated flatly, and The Preacher shrugged.

"Maybe, but we all do what we must to survive and that is why I cannot allow you to live. I am sorry, killing a woman is a dishonourable thing, but you leave me no choice."

He stared at Isabella still on her knees, her head thrown back in fierce resistance, her eyes locked onto his.

Refusing to give him the satisfaction of seeing even a flicker of fear in her face, she stared him down, until at last his eyes dropped and he gestured irritably at one of his men.

"Fetch my daughter," he ordered. "I wish her to witness this." The man hurried to comply. "Get up," he barked, and Isabella slowly complied.

"Despite the fact you are a woman and therefore not entitled to the same niceties of honour that a man is, I will allow you to die on your feet and not on your knees."

"You expect me to thank you for that?" Isabella snarled.

"No, I expect you to make your peace with whatever deity you pray to," he retorted.

"You won't get away with this," Isabella told him, and he shrugged.

"You are a nothing and a nobody. Maybe Nick Eastman did have feelings for you which made him soft. That was a mistake that has cost him his liberty and probably his life. I do not intend to make the same mistake."

"Father?"

The soft voice broke into The Preacher's tirade and Kashm entered the cavern. Crossing to the dais her gaze flicked to Isabella. Horror briefly flashed in her eyes, and she faltered.

It was only for a second, before she recovered herself and turned to face her father, but it was enough.

He noted her reaction to seeing Isabella bound and at his mercy and his paranoia and distrust of everyone – even his daughter – roared to the surface.

"So, you did help them to escape," he demanded fiercely and Kashm shook her head desperately, tears spurting to her cheeks.

"No, no, I promise you, Father, someone locked me in the kitchen. I had no idea what had happened until you let me out."

"You lie!" screamed her father and swung his weapon from his shoulder aiming it at her heart.

"Father," Kashm shrieked in terror and fell to her knees, her hands held out to him.

Around the cavern, the men shifted uneasily exchanging glances and Isabella could almost sense their conflict.

Killing Isabella, an infidel, and a stranger, was one thing, but killing his innocent daughter was something else, and mutterings broke out as the men shuffled.

Some of them though, Isabella noted with disgust, edged forward in excitement, their blood lust aroused at the thought of violence.

"Leave her alone," Isabella shouted. "She had nothing to do with our escape. I locked her in the kitchen so she couldn't interfere."

"You must have had help," The Preacher insisted, his weapon still trained on the terrified Kashm.

"I didn't need any help," Isabella insisted, risking a tiny step forward and then another.

"Nick shot Badih and told me to hide in the goat shed. He gave me a knife, and told me that when it got dark, I was to slash the tyres on all the vehicles except the jeep, and then turn the lights out to cause panic."

"You lie."

"Why? Why should I lie? If I'm about to die, then I don't want to meet my maker with a lie in my heart and the blood of an innocent woman on my hands."

"You are an infidel. A corrupt and faithless Westerner. You would not care, because you believe in nothing but money, and the acquiring of materialistic things."

Around her, Isabella sensed a mood shift in the men – although couldn't tell if it was because of his words – or hers.

"I don't care what you think of me," Isabella told him. "Your daughter did not betray you. She was kind to me, yes, and brought me hot water to wash with as a consideration for my basic needs – woman to woman – but that was all. She did not betray you, and she did not help us to escape."

Conviction rang in Isabella's voice and for a moment, the gun in The Preacher's hand wavered and he looked down on the desperately sobbing figure of his daughter as she rocked in terror on the floor.

"Is this true?" he demanded, and Kashm raised a tear-drenched face to his.

"It is as she says, Father. I took her hot water to wash with, but I would never betray you. You are my Father, and all my obedience and honour must be for you, and you, alone."

The Preacher looked away as if in thought and Isabella took a couple more steps sideways until she was almost at Kashm's side, then he turned and levied a terrible smile onto his daughter.

"You lie," he said calmly, and lifted his weapon and fired.

~Chapter Seventeen~
"You must find him."

Isabella had been expecting it. Something in his eyes, and his stance. That paranoia and the mania that screamed of a man lost to all reason and logic.

Yanking off the handcuffs as she moved, Isabella barged into Kashm, who cried out and clutched at her as the gun spat and The Preacher shot his daughter for her perceived betrayal.

Falling to the ground, Kashm screamed in shock and Isabella bent over her, seeing the blood, and fearing the worst.

Quickly, Isabella assessed the damage – a flesh wound through the soft tissue of the young girl's shoulder – she'd live.

Isabella glanced up at The Preacher posed on the dais like some ancient god intent on meting out vengeance on the mere mortals huddled at his feet.

Well, she'd live for now.

"On your knees," he screamed and brought the gun down to bear on them. "On your knees! You have forfeited the right to an honourable death. Both of you will be put down like the soulless animals you are."

"Father," pleaded Kashm hysterically, as Isabella slipped an arm around the young girl's shaking body and helped her to sit.

"Father, please..."

"I am your father no more. You are dead to me. From this moment on, I am childless."

Kashm sobbed in utter anguish and clutched at Isabella in despair.

"Close your eyes," Isabella urged her. "Hold onto me and close your eyes."

For the briefest of moments, Isabella considered tackling the man nearest her. Even though there were too many for her to get very far, still if she had been alone, Isabella would have rather died on her feet trying to escape than on her knees awaiting her fate.

But she wasn't alone, there was Kashm who was hanging onto her, sobbing with pain and terror, the blood spreading from the wound in her shoulder and her face stricken with what was about to happen.

Isabella couldn't leave her to face it alone, so instead, she drew the young girl to her and turned Kashm's face into her chest.

"Close your eyes," she urged again.

She stared over Kashm's bowed head into the eyes of their murderer. Refusing to make it easy for him, she wanted him to remember to his dying day the disdain in Isabella's eyes when he shot her.

"Close your eyes," he ordered.

"No."

"Close your eyes!"

"Rot in hell, you bastard."

He raised his weapon, and then all hell *did* let loose in the cavern as men in protective armour carrying heavy assault weapons were suddenly there – tackling the stunned followers of The Preacher to the ground and relieving them of their weapons.

"Lay down your gun!"

Isabella gave a great gulp of shocked relief as Sebastian strode into the cavern, bareheaded and completely without armour. Incongruous in his well-cut, expensive Italian suit, his gaze fixed upon the figure of The Preacher.

"Never!" screamed the man who believed himself invincible.

He raised his gun again on the kneeling figures of the women, and Sebastian shot him dead where he stood.

"I don't understand, how did you know where to find me?" Isabella was sitting beside Kashm – who was having her shoulder looked at by a field medic – drinking the cup of excellent coffee her cousin had managed to produce from somewhere.

"Your phone," Sebastian replied. "We were able to find you using the tracking device implanted within it."

"Of course, you did," Isabella replied. "They took it off me when they kidnapped me, I guess I assumed they had abandoned it somewhere in London, but they brought it here with them. I suppose they thought if it were switched off then it couldn't be tracked."

"More fool them," Sebastian said, then laid a concerned hand on her arm. "Are you all right, Isabella?"

"Yes, but we need to go and rescue Nick."

"Nick? Isn't he somewhere amongst that lot?"

Sebastian waved a coolly contemptuous hand at the remnants of The Preacher's followers who were being herded into vans ready for the drive back to Kandahar.

"No, we were wrong about him. Sebastian, he's CIA. Deep undercover trying to gather intel on The Preacher."

"Is he really?" Sebastian's eyebrows rose with surprise. "Well," he considered the matter. "I guess that explains a lot. Good, I'm glad ... for your sake, Isabella."

"You don't understand, oh, it's such a long and complicated story and there's no time. We must get back to the city and rescue him before they have a chance to take him god knows where and we can't find him."

Isabella tipped the dregs of her coffee to the ground and jumped to her feet.

"Kashm," she said, turning to the younger girl who had been silently listening to their conversation.

"The medics are going to take you back to the city, to the hospital there. They need to operate on your shoulder to get the bullet out and repair any damage."

"Please." Kashm gripped her hand in fear. "Please come with me."

"I want to," Isabella replied. "But I have to go and find Nick."

"Yes." Kashm reluctantly released her hand. "You must find him."

"We need to get back to the city asap," Isabella told Sebastian and he nodded.

"We can take my helicopter, and, on the way, you can brief me on everything that has happened over the last four days."

"Is that all it's been?" wondered Isabella. "It feels like an eternity. But we must hurry. We must find him before it's too late."

They were too late. By the time they returned to the city, gathered up a taskforce and raided the home of one Karim Idrissi – he was gone.

Searching the lavish house empty of all but a few terrified servants, they found nothing left of Nick other than his clothes, still lying in Isabella's room and a smattering of his blood on the floor by the front door.

Stunned, unable to believe she had lost him, Isabella fretted as a translator was found to question the servants, but it quickly became apparent they had no idea where their master had gone to, only that he had left in a hurry, leaving instructions to pack up the house and that he would send for them.

Isabella had a feeling that wouldn't be happening anytime soon, that Karim Idrissi had gone to ground somewhere, assuming a new identity and starting afresh.

Sebastian contacted the CIA and agents in Kandahar met with them to debrief Isabella, but their eyes wouldn't meet hers and she knew they believed Nick was dead his body dumped in a grave somewhere, never to be found.

She refused to believe that.

Nick was still alive somewhere she was sure of it; could feel it within her hear.

He was somewhere in the world, just waiting for her to find him.

Visiting Kashm in hospital, Isabella was relieved to learn that the girl's aunt – the sister of her deceased mother – had been located.

Ecstatic that her niece had been found alive, and even happier to discover that her much-despised brother-in-law was dead, Kashm's aunt offered her a loving home.

She had four cousins she knew nothing of, Kashm told Isabella in excitement. Already, they had sent her cards and letters welcoming her to their home.

Happy for the girl, Isabella hugged her fiercely and told her to stay in touch but guessed by the way Kashm's eyes wouldn't meet hers that she would never hear from the young woman again. This part of her life was now over, and Kashm wanted no reminders.

Isabella understood.

She stayed on in Kandahar for a further week, and Sebastian stayed with her. Tracking down any lead, no matter how tenuous, they looked for Nick together.

It was no good.

It was as if Nick Eastman had vanished into thin air.

Eventually, Isabella was forced to return to England with Sebastian. We can continue the search from there, he told her. We won't give up. We will keep on looking until we find him, or...

He didn't finish the sentence; he didn't have to. Isabella knew what he meant.

They would search until they found Nick or proof of his death.

Back home, everything was the same – but everything was different. A powerhouse of commitment, Isabella chivvied and bullied officials and diplomats across the Middle East to make discreet enquiries.

Using every contact at Sebastian's disposal, she shamelessly pulled strings and name-dropped until there were no more leads to follow.

Weeks slipped by … a month … and Isabella knew the trail had gone cold, that the chances of her finding him were slim to zero.

Despair crept into her heart.

Kelly, her number two, proved her mettle in those dark days. Fielding all other demands upon Isabella's time and attention, Kelly took most of her workload onto her shoulders, and Isabella wondered how she would have coped without her.

Staring at the coffee and sandwich the blonde woman had slipped wordlessly onto her desk one evening, Isabella's shoulders slumped in despair.

"I'm never going to find him, am I?"

Kelly paused, looking up from the file she was perusing. Concern at the exhaustion on Isabella's face and the dark shadows under her eye had the younger woman frowning in disapproval.

"You mustn't give up, Isabella. You'll find him, we just have to keep on looking."

"But where? Where do we look, Kelly? The trail has gone cold, no one seems to know anything and I'm all out of options."

"What about talking to the CIA again?"

"I already spoke to their agents in Kandahar. They were no help at all; it's like they'd given up on him."

"You always tell me to go straight to the top," Kelly said. "What is it you always say? Don't speak to the monkey if you want to find something out, always…"

"Speak to the organ grinder," Isabella finished and gazed thoughtfully into space. "Go to the men at the top?" she mused. "Maybe, they would know more. But I don't have the kind of clout to get them to even talk to me."

"Maybe you don't," Kelly replied. "But we both know someone who perhaps does."

~Chapter Eighteen~
"He may already be dead,"

It took three phone calls and some tough talking on Sebastian's part – and possibly even promises of future favours owed – before Nick's handler in the CIA and his superior agreed to fly to London to meet with them.

Despite their steely-eyed countenance and firm jaws, Isabella wondered how much help they would be.

"Look," Nick's handler began. "We regret the loss of Nick Eastman. He was a good agent, and over the five years he's been with the Agency he's done some outstanding work."

"And yet you just gave up on him," Isabella snapped, and the older man sighed.

"We didn't give up on him, but without a solid lead on where to look, we don't even have a place to start. We checked out this Karim Idrissi and he's totally in the wind – probably snuggled up in a new home somewhere under a new identity. The man had the funds to simply disappear."

"You have to try," Isabella pressed. "We have no idea what's happening to Nick, he could be being tortured, he could be dying, he…"

Her voice trailed away and the oldest man in the room, the big noise from the CIA finally spoke, a hint of rough sympathy in his voice.

"Look, Miss Santorini, we do understand. But the truth is we simply don't have enough eyes on the ground in Europe and the Middle East to even stand a chance of finding him. If we had more manpower to mount an international search, we would, but we don't."

"You may not," said Isabella, an idea breaking in her mind. "But I know someone who does."

Agreeing immediately to do anything within his power to help, Luke Blackwood, and his trusty second-in-command, James Sullivan, dropped everything and met with them that afternoon.

As the burly men crowded into the conference room, Isabella instantly felt more hopeful, their mere presence enough to raise her spirits.

Luke was married to her sister-in-law, Arianna, and so he was family.

Sullivan was married to Luke's sister, Susannah, and as far as Isabella was concerned, that meant he was family as well.

Owner of ICRA – the International Child Recovery Agency – Luke had been instrumental in finding Isabella's niece, Lucia, when she had been snatched by her father – Isabella's brother, Roberto – and whisked away to South America.

Refusing to leave any stone unturned in his quest to recover her, Luke finally brought Lucia home to her mother, and the woman Luke loved – Arianna.

Isabella trusted Luke, knew he was good at what he did, knew he had a network of informers and agents across the world, that he could very well be the 'eyes on the ground' the CIA claimed they lacked.

Briefly, Sebastian brought both men up to speed and Luke shook his head in thought, looking at Isabella with sympathy.

"No wonder we haven't seen much of you lately," was all he said, and turned to the CIA agents.

"What leads do we have?" he asked, and Isabella knew instantly that he would do this for her. Without question, without thought, just because he knew how important it was to her, he would put ICRA's vast resources at her disposal to find one man.

"Everything we have is in this file," Nick's handler replied and passed over a slim buff folder. "There isn't much, I'm afraid. With no clue as to where Idrissi took him or why then there's not much to go on."

"Wait a minute," Isabella stared at them in confusion, a frown pulling at her forehead. "What do you mean, we don't know why he took him? What about this Sullivan person Karim said he was giving him to? Did you check him out?"

"Sullivan?" said Luke and the handler together, and Luke glanced at Jimmy Sullivan who shrugged his shoulders.

"Nothing to do with me," he murmured.

"What Sullivan person?" the handler asked. "There's nothing about it in the file."

"Damn." Isabella cursed the lackadaisical attitude and sloppy paperwork of the agents in Kandahar, but most of all cursed herself for not going higher up the CIA food chain sooner.

"I told your agents about him in Afghanistan," she snapped, not caring if she was throwing them under the bus.

"Karim told me that he was in debt to someone much bigger than him, someone very important. He said this someone had wanted revenge on Nick for five years. He said his name, it sounded like Sullivan, but it might have been something that sounded like that."

The two CIA men exchanged swift glances.

"What?" Isabella demanded. "That means something to you, doesn't it? Who is he?"

"Is it possible the name was Suliman?" one asked and Isabella nodded in quick excitement.

"Yes, that was it. Suliman. Who is he?"

"He's one of the wealthiest men in Saudi Arabia. Think oil, and it will probably have Suliman's name stamped on the barrels. We've long suspected that he crosses lines when it comes to business deals and human rights, but never had anything to pin on him."

"Why would he want Nick Eastman?" Sebastian asked in interest.

"Suliman's son, Ahmad, was a loose cannon," Nick's handler began. "Typical spoilt rich brat. Used to daddy's money and name getting him out of numerous scrapes. His father eventually sent him to Yale University in the hopes it would steady him down and prepare him for taking over the family firm, but it didn't quite work out how daddy hoped."

His colleague took over the story.

"Ahmed liked to walk on the rough side and got involved in a gang of petty criminals who robbed a string of gas stations and mom and pop stores in the area. I think it was just a joke to Ahmed, a way of letting off steam, but something went wrong, and a 65-year-old grandfather ended up being shot and killed by Ahmed."

"What happened to Ahmed?" Isabella asked.

"Nick was still working on the force then, and he was the one who arrested Ahmed. But Suliman played the diplomatic immunity card and arrangements were made to ship his son back to Saudi Arabia."

The man sighed and spread his hands in disgusted resignation at a system that let people off murder because of money and power.

"Before that could happen, Ahmed got into a fight in detention and was stabbed to death. I remember it caused a massive stink at the time that rumbled on for years."

"And Suliman blamed Nick for it," Isabella said. "Even though he was just doing his job, it was still his fault that Ahmed was in a position to be killed. But why has he waited so long?"

"Nick Eastman was recruited into the CIA soon after and has spent most of the past five years on one undercover mission after another. He would have been hard to locate."

"Until now," Sebastian finished. "Somehow, Idrissi heard the story and offered Nick to Suliman in exchange for wiping out his debts."

They all looked at each other, hope suddenly rising between them.

"It's a place to start," Isabella said, and the other men nodded.

"It is," the older CIA man said. "It's a definite place to start."

With the combined forces of the CIA, ICRA, and Sebastian's organisation, information about Suliman soon began to flood in. An extremely wealthy man, he and his family lived in luxury on a substantial compound just outside Riyadh.

"He would want to have Nick close," Isabella stated. "To gloat over him. Nick imprisoned his son, so now it's his turn to imprison him."

"He may already be dead." Nick's handler worried.

"No," Isabella said. "Suliman wanted revenge and he's had five long years to plan it. To kill him so quickly, that's not satisfying at all. No, he'll want to draw it out, to make Nick suffer…"

Her voice trailed away at the thought of what Nick might be going through, and Sebastian dropped a hand onto her shoulder in sympathy.

"Isabella is right," he said. "The revenge culture is strong in these countries, and I think a quick death wouldn't satisfy Suliman. No, he'll want Nick alive and paying for his son's death every single day."

The door banged open, and Luke hurried in clutching a file, Sullivan on his heels.

"We think we've found a possible location," he declared, and the others leant forward in anticipation as he slapped the file onto the table.

"During the Cold War, Suliman's father had a nuclear bunker built close to his home. Since the fall of the Berlin Wall, it's been abandoned, but my agents in Riyadh have reported activity. Vans with guards and supplies are regularly paying visits, and even Suliman himself has been out there. This is very unusual, and I think it means…"

"That Nick is being held captive in this bunker," Isabella finished with conviction.

"Possibly," Luke said, then nodded slowly. "But I think you may be right. There's no reason for this sudden renewed activity in an old, abandoned bunker unless there is now something there of interest."

"It's Nick! What else could it be?" Isabella demanded again.

"Okay." The CIA agent looked at Luke's files with interest. "Trouble is, we have no jurisdiction in Saudi Arabia, and going through the proper channels to gain the clearance necessary could tip Suliman off. By the time we could do something, he would have moved Eastman to a new location, and we'd be starting from nowhere again, less than nowhere."

"It might even spook him into killing Nick," his handler interjected in concern.

"I don't know what else we can do." His superior threw his hands up in despair. "We can't storm in, all guns blazing."

"You have to do something!" Isabella demanded. "We have a real chance of finding Nick, the only chance we may ever get. And because you're too scared of upsetting your oil supplies, you're not going to do anything!"

"Lady, I don't like it any more than you do," the CIA agent snapped in exasperated frustration. "But my hands are tied."

"Maybe yours are," Sebastian interrupted smoothly. "But my hands aren't."

The CIA men stared at him.

"We operate outside the jurisdiction of any country or government. We can go in, extract Nick, and be out before anyone is the wiser. Once we have him, Suliman will know the game is up and then diplomatic pressure can be brought to bear upon him to ensure he never tries to take Nick again."

"Okay," the CIA supervisor said. "But I know nothing about it. This whole conversation must have occurred when I was out of the room."

"I'm going with you," Nick's handler suddenly stated, and at the enquiring look of his superior looked sheepish. "Nick's a good guy, he doesn't deserve this. You can say I was on vacation or something, but I'm going."

"So am I," stated Luke, and beside him, James Sullivan nodded.

"Count me in."

"I'm going too," Isabella stated, and Nick's handler looked pained.

"Lady, this isn't a Sunday School picnic," he growled. "You could get hurt, and I for one don't want to have to babysit you."

In a movement so fast none of them saw it, the man's head hit the desk and his arm was being held behind his back at a painful angle by Isabella. She bent close to his face which was grimacing in shocked pain.

"I don't need anyone to babysit me," she hissed in his ear and released him.

Straightening up, the man rubbed at his numb shoulder and looked around ruefully at the circle of grinning male faces.

"Guess she's coming too," he mumbled.

~Chapter Nineteen~
"He was a nobody."

Confusing images of Isabella fighting what looked like a dozen men at once. A last glimpse of her beautiful face covered in blood as she was dragged past him in handcuffs.

Her voice calling his name ... and then nothing.

When the fog finally lifted, he was bound, gagged, and blindfolded, and he was on a plane – at least, he thought he was.

His stomach lurched in symphony with the familiar feel of the dipping of a light aircraft.

Yes, he was on a plane.

Slowly memory came back.

Karim had drugged and betrayed him.

Isabella had been right not to trust the man, and Nick cursed his stupidity in not listening to her.

Isabella.

He wondered where she was; if she was all right, the thought of anything bad happening to her made his guts roil even more.

He shifted to ease the cramp in his hip and tried to ignore the ache of an overfull bladder. He wondered where he was and who was holding him prisoner and struggled to remember what Karim said as the drug pulled him under.

Had he said Suliman?

A memory stirred at the name and Nick poked at it, trying to trigger the recollection.

Yes, Ahmed Suliman, that rich Saudi kid who had gotten a little trigger happy during a robbery and killed the shopkeeper.

Scheduled to be quietly shipped back to his influential father who had pulled diplomatic immunity, the dumb kid threw his weight around in detention, pissed off the wrong people, and ended up getting shived in the shower.

But what did that have to do with him?

Yes, he had been the arresting officer, but he'd only been doing his job.

Nick had a nasty feeling about the situation, and it – together with hunger, a raging thirst, his cramped limbs, and a need to pee that was getting beyond mere urgency – kept him awake and worried for the rest of the journey.

They unloaded him none too gently, pushed him into some sort of holding cell, and removed the gag and blindfold.

Stark and unfurnished, at least the room contained a working toilet, and they did give him food and water.

They were near an airport; he was sure of that much. The rumble of jets taking off and landing regularly shook the small room.

But that was the only thing he was sure of.

After a couple of hours, they came for him. Once again, he was gagged and blindfolded, then roughly pushed to shuffle a few steps as best he could in the leg irons.

Hands then yanked him up into a truck and he was unceremoniously shoved down onto the floor.

They drove for no more than an hour or so, then he was unloaded and forced to hobble a few steps in blazing sunlight, beating down on his exposed head.

Then they were indoors again, hands removing his blindfold and gag. He looked around curiously.

Some sort of base.

Military?

Possibly, it had the abandoned, utilitarian feel of old military installations.

His eyes constantly moving to take in every detail, he was forced to make his way slowly down a flight of metal steps that appeared to lead into the very bowels of the earth.

Bomb shelter?

That seemed more likely.

But where?

Glancing at his escort he noted their swarthy complexions. The Middle East somewhere. Suliman was Saudi, was Nick now in Saudi Arabia?

It was possible, he supposed. The flight time from Kandahar to Riyadh – where he remembered Suliman lived – was approximately ten hours.

Depending on how long he'd been unconscious, the timing would fit.

Eventually, they reached the bottom of the stairs and Nick was shoved through a door into a small room empty of furniture except for a desk and a chair at which Suliman sat, his eyes glinting with feral anticipation at the sight of Nick – bound and helpless.

"Mr Eastman," he purred, looking Nick up and down. "We meet at last."

Nick's lips twitched as a wild urge to laugh nearly overwhelmed him.

Who did this guy think he was? A bad Bond villain?

"I assume you're Suliman?" he asked, and the fake smile dropped from the other man's face.

"Yes, I am Ahmed Suliman's father, and I have been waiting for this moment for a very long time."

"Look," said Nick, in as rational a tone as he could manage. "I'm sorry about your son, but I was only doing my job."

"Doing your job? My son was butchered in a barbaric American prison because of you."

"Be reasonable," Nick said. "He had murdered someone, an innocent old man who'd done him no harm – your son shot him down in cold blood, and for what? A joke, a lark."

"He was a nobody."

Suliman dismissed the shopkeeper's demise with an airy wave of his hand.

"My son – my only son – was destined for great things. He was being groomed to take over from me, but because of you his life was over before it had even had a chance to begin."

Nick's heart sank at the maniacal gleam in the other man's eyes.

Like Isabella when she confronted The Preacher, he realised he faced a man for whom normal considerations did not apply.

Wealthy beyond belief, privileged from birth, and unable to accept that other people had the same rights as himself, Suliman was a dangerous man and Nick was completely at his mercy.

"I am sorry about your son," he said, sincerity in his voice. "But I was only doing my duty, what I was ordered to do."

"The excuse of mindless fools throughout history," Suliman scoffed. "It was unacceptable in 1946 and it is unacceptable now."

"So, you kill me," Nick shrugged. "How does that help your son? It won't bring him back."

"Oh, Mr Eastman."

Suliman leaned over the desk towards him, his eyes glittering with intense satisfaction.

"I am not going to kill you, although you may wish I had."

After that, Nick was taken to another room even deeper underground.

A room the clean light of day would never touch. A room no bigger than the average bathroom.

His chains were taken off, he was shoved roughly inside, and the thick blast door was closed behind him.

He had brief moments to scan his surroundings before the lights switched off and he was left in darkness.

Complete and utter darkness.

Hours passed. Or it could have been days. With no light and no way to tell the passing of time, it merged and blended into one constant stream of simply being.

The only break in the monotony was when the door briefly opened, and a tray of food and water was pushed through.

They left him to stew for a while, and then the whippings began.

Dragged from his cell at gunpoint he would be marched to another room where the rack awaited him.

Chained to it, he would wait for what he knew was coming.

A lash.

Thin and stingingly painful. It was enough to hurt and demoralise, but not enough to seriously wound or kill.

No, Nick soon understood that it was to humiliate him, to appease Suliman's twisted appetite for vengeance.

Biting his lip to stop himself from crying out, Nick was aware the whole time of Suliman sitting in the corner on a chair watching the torture.

Never speaking, barely reacting, he would simply sit there and watch.

Only the gleam in his dark eyes and the increased rise and fall of his chest beneath his snowy white pristine robes, revealed his intense pleasure at seeing his enemy so brought down.

The whippings were not regular, but random. Sometimes twice in what seemed a very short time, and then the lash would flail at tender flesh which had not had a chance to begin healing.

Other times it felt days had passed before the door was thrown open and he was once more dragged out into the light.

Nick almost welcomed the whippings. For when he was hanging on the rack, at least he was in the light.

Left alone for so long in the dark, Nick felt his grip on sanity beginning to slip. His back ripped to shreds and sticky with blood, he would lie face down on the floor and drift in a fugue state in which images and happenings from his past drifted through his mind in a confusing collage of fact and fiction.

There were rats in his cell.

He could hear them rustling and squeaking in the corners. Once, trying to grope for his food bowl in the dark, he felt a furry body crouched on it and yelped as the rat sank its sharp teeth into his hand.

Untreated, the wound festered and for days Nick lay in a fever until the door was thrown open and they dragged him out for his usual whipping.

Frowning at the state of him, Suliman ordered he be given antibiotics and that his wound be cleaned and dressed.

Then he ordered him whipped and thrown back into his cell.

And so, it went on, and on, until Nick lost all touch with reality and almost accepted that this was his life.

Almost, but not quite.

One thing anchored him to the man he had been. One face swam regularly before his eyes. Her voice telling him to hold on, that she was coming for him, but that he had to hold on.

Isabella.

Logically, Nick knew it to be impossible Isabella could ever find him. How would she even know where to begin looking?

Yet still, he hoped.

Desperately he ignored the voices in his head whispering that Isabella was probably dead. Instead, he chose to trust in his heart that beat fiercely with the knowledge she was very much alive.

Isabella could not be dead, because how could he still be alive if she were no more?

But eventually, as time slipped by in slow, trickling moments – measured by the endless whippings and the steady thud of his heartbeat – even the hope that was Isabella began to fade, until there were only tattered shreds remaining of what had once been Nick Eastman.

~Chapter Twenty~
"Want to go for a ride?"

He noticed her at once – how could he not. With her long dark hair flowing over her shoulders, her beautiful strong face, and the tanned lithe body showcased in shorts and a pretty, blue top, she was every teenage boy's dream of an Italian babe.

But it was more than that. As he worked his tables and rushed to collect orders from the harassed chef in the roasting hot kitchen, Nick's eyes constantly slid to where she sat, slowly sipping a cold lemonade.

Imagining that she was watching him, he stole nervous glances to where she sat alone, at a table out on the patio. Yet every time he glanced her way, her face was turned toward the sea.

Her eyes hidden behind dark glasses, he couldn't tell if she was watching him or not, but the idea she might be had his suddenly clammy hands fumbling a plate of food and almost dropping it. Reddening at the good-natured joshing of Luigi the chef and the other waiters, Nick pulled himself together and hurried to deliver the order.

Desperately trying to keep up with the lunchtime rush, the next time he looked at her, she had finished her drink and was gone.

After his shift, he slipped out of the kitchen and headed to where he left his motorbike, only to find her sitting on the wall, waiting for him.

He stopped and stared at her.

She had taken the glasses off and was even more beautiful than he imagined. Her dark eyes coolly examining him, as if seeing into his soul.

"Hello," he said, and she smiled.

With a slow lifting of the corners of her mouth, her full lips dipped into a crescent that showed a glimpse of perfect white teeth.

"Hello," she replied in English, although the Italian accent was there.

"I saw you earlier," he said. Then cursed himself for the deeply uncool, stalker-like comment.

"I know," she said. "I saw you too."

For a moment they simply looked at one another, caught in the agony of teenage mutual attraction, then she gestured at the motorbike.

"Is this yours?"

"Yes," he replied. "I'm travelling around Europe on it for my gap year."

She nodded in admiration.

"I have never been on one," she admitted, and, on a whim, he held out his helmet to her.

"Want to go for a ride?" he asked.

And that was where it began. The story that was Nick and Isabella. He tried to keep it casual, aware that he would not be staying long in this sleepy Italian coastal town and not wishing to risk breaking her heart, or his own.

But it was impossible to contain. His heart and head were so full of her there was no space for anything else.

The other waiters teased but understood. Red-blooded Italian males all raised in the art of romance; they gave him advice that he mostly ignored.

Laughing at how completely he had fallen, they encouraged and were even complicit in keeping their affair secret.

Because it *had* to be kept secret. Isabella's family were wealthy and influential. There were obligations Isabella would be expected to fulfil, obligations that did not include a penniless American boy with no connections or future.

When her brother grew suspicious of the amount of time she was spending at the restaurant, the other waiters covered for them.

Lying to Roberto's face, they spun a fabrication of a group of English girls that his sister had been spending a lot of time with.

A little wild maybe, but a harmless bunch of nice girls on holiday in the sun. Isabella was just having a little teenage fun with them, blowing off some steam. Apparently satisfied with the story, Roberto went away.

Quite why Isabella was so afraid of her brother, she would never explain. Nick only knew she was and feared for her.

He also knew that should her parents ever find out about them, he would be banned from her life, and as that prospect was unthinkable, he played along with her paranoia about her family.

Anything, to keep her with him.

They were careful not to be seen together. Meeting out on the road, she would tuck her long hair up into the helmet and climb onto the back of his motorbike. Feeling her slim arms wrapped around him, he would drive them to deserted coves and places along the coast where they could be together.

When he told her he loved her, she smiled and said – "I know" – then became confused when he laughed at the famous Star Wars reference.

She had never seen any of the films, she told him. Don't bother, he replied. The Empire Strikes Back is the only one worth watching.

And then they became lovers.

It was as inevitable as the turning of the planet that she would creep out of her house one night and climb up the ivy to the balcony of the room he was renting for the season.

He was waiting for her, and when she fell into his arms giggling with nervous disbelief at what she had done, he thought his heart would burst with happiness.

After that, there was no question of his leaving. He had made no firm plans, had no one expecting him so could linger in this town by the sea that was beginning to feel like home.

They talked about everything.

She told him of her longing for a little home of her own – somewhere truly hers where she could feel safe and protected. A fierce desire to provide her with such a place burned within him.

He shared with her his passion for writing, of his plans to publish a novel someday, even allowing her to read some of his work. He watched in pretended casual disinterest as she turned the pages and quietly read his words.

They are beautiful, she told him. She knew that one day he would be a great writer, and his heart burned at the strength of her faith in him.

He would bring leftovers home from the restaurant, and they would lie on his bed after making sweet, innocent love, hungrily consuming them with the greed of the young.

We go together like meatballs and spaghetti, he told her, and she laughed at the idea.

Then she told him of the English people who were coming to visit. They had a daughter of Isabella's age, but she was at school and would not be coming with them – this time.

There was an understanding between them and Isabella's parents that maybe, in time, and if the young couple liked one another, that Isabella's brother Roberto and this young English girl, Arianna, would marry.

Stunned at the idea of an arranged marriage in this day and age, the notion occurred to Nick that such an understanding also existed for Isabella. He questioned her, fear making his voice harsh.

Yes, she agreed sadly. Her family would put pressure on her to marry whomever they chose. A nice respectable boy from a wealthy and important Italian family. But she wouldn't, she insisted fiercely, seeing the fear on his face. She loved only him, would not allow anything to come between them.

And so, the English people came to stay, and Isabella couldn't spend all day away from home anymore but had to be with her parents and her brother as they made their guests welcome.

Although the nights still belonged to them.

Every evening, Isabella would slip from the house and run the short distance down to the town to climb into his room. Spending the night in blissful denial in his arms, she would creep back as dawn was breaking over the sea, and no one ever knew.

No one ever suspected – or so they thought.

Then, on the last day of their visit, the nice English couple went for a plane ride with Isabella's parents – and none of them came back.

As he tried to comfort Isabella who was prostrate with grief, a tiny voice whispered inside Nick's head that now there was no one to force Isabella to marry.

They were safe.

She was his and his completely.

Hating himself for the nasty thought, Nick fiercely pushed it away and devoted himself to caring for the girl he loved.

Gradually, over the weeks that followed the double funeral, Nick noticed a change in Isabella.

Always concerned about keeping their relationship a secret, now she became paranoid to the point of hysteria.

When finally, he confronted her about it, she broke down and confessed how afraid she had become of her brother, Roberto.

There had never been any love lost between them, and Isabella had hinted at wrongs and hurts visited on her by the older and controlling Roberto, but now she seemed genuinely terrified of him – of what he might do to her.

Roberto had spoken of a school he was thinking of sending her to, a finishing school far, far away in the Swiss Alps, where she would stay until after her eighteenth birthday.

Unable to bear the thought of being parted, plans were conceived. When Nick left the town to move on to the next destination on his European tour, Isabella would go with him.

It was the perfect scheme, she insisted. She had money of her own so wouldn't be a burden.

They could slip away one night, and no one would know where they had gone.

So long as they rode far enough away and were careful, they could remain hidden until Isabella's eighteenth birthday in six months and then it wouldn't matter.

Once she came of age, Isabella explained, she would come into her inheritance. Her brother's guardianship of her would be at an end and Isabella would be able to make her own choices.

They would be free to be together.

It was decided.

Nick gave in his notice at the restaurant with some regret. The people there had been good to him, and he would genuinely miss them.

Covering his tracks, he named a town some miles to the South as his next destination, when in fact he and Isabella planned to travel North. Making sure he gave the same information to his landlady, he packed up his motorbike and set off in the inky blackness of a perfect Italian evening to collect Isabella as pre-arranged.

He waited for her.

She never came.

Instead, her brother sauntered out of the moonlight bearing news that struck the young man a blow he never quite recovered from.

Isabella wasn't coming, Roberto told him. She had sent her brother to apologise. At the last minute, she'd reconsidered and realised that throwing her future away on a nobody was a foolish idea.

Then he gave Nick a letter that broke his heart when he read it and crushed the pieces still further with every re-reading.

The letter was in Isabella's distinctive looped handwriting. If Nick had had any doubt about that he would have ridden up to the house and demanded to see her, wanting to hear her say those cruel words herself.

Leave, Roberto told him. Go, before he called the authorities down onto him with an accusation of rape.

Ignoring Nick's indignant protestations of innocence, Roberto dealt him the final blow and gave him back the locket he had bought Isabella many weeks before.

Glinting in the light of the full moon, it mocked his pain, and he was tempted to throw it into the sea. But he didn't; he tucked it into his jacket pocket and roared away into the night.

His heart breaking with the full anguish of a teenage love that felt so true but had been as flimsy and ephemeral as the summer breeze.

A month later, he would pull the locket from his pocket for the first time and frown at the snapped chain.

Examining it closely, he realised the violence of the yank it must have taken to completely snap and twist the sturdy clasp and noticed what looked like a minute smear of blood encrusted into the links. Putting it away, he determined to think no more of it.

But it niggled and nagged at his mind and would not let him be, until finally, he climbed onto his motorbike and rode back to that little town by the sea.

He was too late.

The house was locked with a sold sign hanging on the front gate. The family were all gone, he was told, moved to England never to return.

He hung around the town for a few days more, making enquiries and hoping for news. But no one knew exactly where the family had gone, and so eventually he sold his bike and used the money to buy a one-way plane ticket home.

Because what else was he to do?

And then he got on with the rest of his life.

He thought he was doing a good job of it until the day Isabella Santorini walked back into his world and he realised he still loved her.

That he had never stopped loving her. That he would love her until the day he died.

Opening his eyes to the pitch dark and the scamper of tiny feet over his body, Nick Eastman felt the hopelessness threaten to engulf him, and his hand groped for the locket.

Fearing, probably correctly, that they would take it away from him if they found it – and unable to bear the thought – Nick had hidden it in the folds of the single blanket they gave him to sleep on.

Every time he heard the door begin to open; he would tuck it away. At Karim's house, he meant to give it back to Isabella but forgot about it. It remained in the pocket of his fatigues that he had pulled on under the clean clothes he was given.

Uncomfortable not wearing anything under the loose flowing robes, he decided the fatigues weren't too bad, and at the last minute had yanked them back on.

The locket was his talisman, his touchstone. Unable to see it, his fingers had traced its delicate carvings so many times they were committed to memory.

The photo of Isabella as she had been that summer he didn't need to see; her image was already etched in his mind.

Again, and again, on an endless loop, their story played out behind his eyes, and each time Nick would awaken to the darkness and feel his face wet with tears.

Isabella.

He whispered her name in the darkness and prayed for death to take him.

~Chapter Twenty-One~
"The man is broken,"

Occasionally, Isabella wondered how extensive Sebastian's influence was, but as their plane approached King Khalid airport, she realised it was considerable.

Taking over the comms, Sebastian spoke to someone and issued a code. Five minutes later they were given clearance to land at a small runway away from the main airport terminal.

Stretching her legs after the long flight, Isabella followed the others over to the dark van awaiting them. A man stood there dressed in unrelieved black combats, his swarthy complexion snapping into an expression of deference at the sight of Sebastian.

"Sir," he said, and Sebastian nodded in reply.

"Report."

"Sir, we have been watching the target and there has been a definite increase in activity. There is a small contingent of Suliman's private guard permanently stationed there, and Suliman himself has been making visits."

"Any pattern to those visits?"

"None, Sir, they appear random."

"Is he there now?"

"Yes, Sir."

"Good." Sebastian smiled coldly. "I have the facts of life to explain to Mr Suliman. Let's go."

Wondering what on earth Sebastian meant by *that*, Isabella remained silent and climbed into the back of the van with the others.

Leaving the airport, the van wove through traffic and was soon heading out into the desert. Jouncing over the rough terrain, Isabella glanced at the others, all dressed like her in black combats, her heart beating so loudly with anticipation she marvelled they didn't hear it.

The drive passed in silence and then they were there. A high link wire fence surrounded a nondescript door into a squat concrete bump in the ground and the van pulled up outside the gates.

"Get us in," Sebastian ordered, and two agents leapt from the van with bolt cutters. A moment later the gates swung open, and the van drove up to the door.

A luxurious stretch limo was parked by the door, and a gleam of satisfaction sparked in Sebastian's eyes, but he said nothing.

Piling from the van, Isabella pulled out her weapon as did the others, her pulse racing with sick excitement.

Trying the door and finding it unlocked, Sebastian raised his brows at the others.

"Obviously not expecting company," he murmured. "You two, keep this exit secure."

"Sir." The two men took up position either side of the door.

It was gloomy inside, the only illumination, emergency lights set at regular intervals in the wall and leading down the flight of metal stairs stretching away into the murky depths.

Down they went in grim silence, senses on red alert, straining for any sign of resistance. Reaching the bottom, the stairs ended in a corridor that stretched away for a few metres before culminating in a thick door of solid concrete at the far end. The door stood open, and Sebastian tutted under his breath.

"Sloppy," he commented, and Luke grinned at him in agreement.

"Love it when they make our job easier."

"You two." Sebastian gestured to Sullivan and another agent. "Make sure this door remains open. It appears the only way in or out and we don't want to be trapped down here."

Isabella shuddered inside at the thought and tried not to imagine what Nick had gone through trapped down here the past six weeks.

The diminished group, now comprising Sebastian, Luke, Isabella, the CIA agent, and two more of Sebastian's men, crept stealthily through the door and down the long corridor beyond.

Room after room they passed. Some were empty, some contained shelves and were meant for storage. Incongruously, one contained a luxurious bathroom and Sebastian shook his head at the sight.

"The world may have gone to shit above you, but that's no excuse to let standards slip," he muttered. They passed more empty rooms which Isabella looked at with wonder.

"You could hide an army down here," she mused, and Luke grinned at her.

"I think that was the point."

They reached a bend in the corridor and Sebastian held up his hand. They stopped.

Cocking his ear, he glanced at them in enquiry and Isabella nodded. She heard it too.

A swish, swish noise that she couldn't place. Each swish accompanied by a wet thud. She looked at Luke who was staring at Sebastian with an expression of horror.

Suddenly, there were noises up ahead – the sound of a door opening. The harsh voices of men and the sound of something, or someone, being dragged. Another door banged, and then booted feet rang out on the concrete floor as the men approached their position.

Risking a glance around the corner, Luke looked at Isabella and held up two fingers. She nodded and pressed her back against the wall, poised to strike. Two men turned the corner and instantly Isabella grabbed the man closest to her, twisted him onto her hip and slammed his head against the wall.

An expression of intense surprise on his face, he slid down it to lay in a crumpled heap at the base. Isabella looked across at Luke who had silenced his man just as effectively.

"Definitely sloppy," she said.

Creeping down the hallway they were faced with two final doors, one on the left and one on the right. The left-hand door was slightly ajar, whilst the right-hand one was shut firm.

Indicating with a tilt of his head that they were to take the open door, the CIA agent and Luke positioned themselves, then with one swift kick the door burst open, and they were in – to find Suliman scrambling up from the table in utter shock, his eyes widening at their combat apparel and heavy-duty weaponry.

"Guards," he yelled. "Guards!"

"Don't bother calling for help," Sebastian told him, stepping coolly into the room followed by Isabella. "None is coming."

Isabella's eyes flicked around the room, at the blood-splattered rack, the evil-looking whip lying on the floor, and her eyes met those of Luke in a moment of shared horror.

"Santorini," the other man spat, his face purple with rage. "What are you doing here?"

"We've come for Nick Eastman."

"Who?" Suliman shrugged, and Sebastian rolled his eyes in exasperation.

"Don't waste my time," he snapped. "We know you took him, we know why, and we know you are holding him here to appease your medieval ideas of revenge and honour."

"He caused my son's death," Suliman roared.

"Your son caused his own death," Sebastian countered, a tone of almost boredom in his voice. "Now, hand Eastman over so we can all go home. Although, I think you may have to wait until your guards wake up unless you fancy driving that gas guzzler out there yourself."

"You won't get away with this, Santorini," Suliman snarled, and Sebastian sighed in amused resignation.

"The leaders of your beautiful country signed an agreement that I can 'get away' with acts like this whenever I choose – in exchange for certain *services* that my organisation provides – services that they have frequently taken advantage of."

Suliman sank back into his chair, frustration twisting his features.

"Now then, what do you think they will do if I inform them that those *services* are no longer available to them because of your actions."

Suliman thought about it and from the look on his face, realised the consequences.

"Take him," he ordered. "I have exacted my revenge anyway. The man is broken. Even though he lives he will never be the same again."

"Bastard," Isabella could contain herself no longer and raised her weapon. "Where is he?"

Suliman jerked his head towards the door and Isabella moved. But swift as she was, Luke was quicker and stopped her at the door.

"Isabella don't ..." he said, and Isabella stared at him in astonishment.

"What do you mean?" she demanded and pushed his hand away. "Nick is in that room; we have to get him out."

"And we will," Luke promised. "But ..." He hesitated and looked to Sebastian for help.

"Whatever we find in that room, Isabella," Sebastian said. "It's not going to be pretty."

"I don't care about that," Isabella growled.

"No, but Nick will. Trust us, Isabella. He won't want you to see him like that."

"They're right," the CIA agent interrupted in agreement. "If this asshole is telling the truth and Nick is broken, then he won't want you to see him like that."

"But..."

"Think about it Isabella," Sebastian urged. "When he recovers, if he knows you saw him like that, then he may never be able to move past it and it could affect your relationship forever."

She thought about it, then savagely kicked the door and the men knew she realised they were right.

"Go and wait in the van," Sebastian told her. "And we'll bring him out."

Isabella nodded then looked at him.

"Just ... just ... look after him."

"We will," Sebastian promised. "Now go."

She went back to the van, informing Sullivan and the other agents on the way that the mission had been successful. They had located Nick and were now bringing him out.

In Sullivan's eyes, she thought she saw understanding, and, briefly, his hand dropped to her shoulder as he nodded.

Then she climbed up the stairs and out into the harsh sunlight. Climbing into the back of the van she sat down and pulled off her helmet.

She wanted to cry.

But that was ridiculous because she was Isabella Santorini and she never cried. The last time had been over eleven years ago, when she had lain on the floor of her bedroom and heard Nick's motorbike, as he roared away into the night thinking she had betrayed him.

So now she swallowed it down, took a swig of water from her canister and waited for them to bring him out to her.

It seemed to take forever, but finally, the group appeared in the doorway, Luke and Sebastian supporting the hunched figure shuffling slowly forward in their midst.

Gently, the men half led, half carried him to the van and helped him in and onto one of the benches that ran along each side.

Isabella could smell him. The stench of a body long uncared for and unwashed, of human waste and rat urine. But most of all, the rank bitter odour of fear and despair.

Not allowing herself to react, she slid along the bench until she was next to him. Dressed only in the fatigues he'd been wearing at Karim's; a blanket had been wrapped around his shoulders.

He sat, bent over, his gaze fixed on his feet. Looking down, Isabella saw they were bruised and bloodied, the skin broken with the lacerations of torture.

Horrified, she glanced up at Luke who was sitting on the other side of Nick, his expression one of tight-lipped fury. He met Isabella's stare and silently shook his head. *You don't want to know*, his eyes said, but Isabella did want to know, wanted to know every awful detail.

There was something clutched in Nick's hand. Gently, Isabella slid her hand over his and softly prised his fingers apart to see.

It was her locket.

Now, Isabella couldn't hold back the single tear that slid down her cheek and she slipped her fingers through his, feeling the skin rough beneath hers and seeing the ripped and blackened fingernails.

For a moment Nick didn't respond, and then his fingers tightened over hers and they sat that way in silence all the way back to the airport.

~Chapter Twenty-Two~
"I'm not worth crying for,"

───────◆•◆───────

They took off immediately, the plane having taken on fuel and prepared for departure whilst they were gone. Once on board, Nick curled up into a ball in his seat and fell asleep. Sitting for a while, watching the rise and fall of his chest under the blanket he clutched like a lifeline, Isabella waited until he was completely under before sliding across to sit next to Luke.

"I want to know," she said.

"Trust me, you don't."

"You think I can't handle it?"

"I know *you* can handle it." Luke nodded soberly towards the huddled man sleeping opposite. "I'm not sure he could, though."

"He will never know you told me. I'll never breathe a word of it to him, but I must know."

"Okay." Luke gave a deep sigh of resignation. "When we opened the door, it was black in there, I mean, totally. I would imagine they've kept him like that the whole time – except when they took him out to whip him."

Isabella nodded; her expression fixed.

"He was lying on the floor, on a filthy blanket, and that was all that was in the room. Just that blanket on a concrete floor. When we went in, he was face down, because his back was in shreds.

Isabella, what they've done to him, it goes beyond mere torture..."

Again, she nodded, unable to speak.

"We turned on the lights and he cried out ... I think the light hurt his eyes. I crouched down and spoke to him, but he was unresponsive and curled up in a ball away from me, but then, I guess he doesn't know me."

"Yet," Isabella ground out. "He doesn't know you yet, but he will, because ... because ... he's going to be part of our family."

"I figured that." Luke smiled, then his face dropped. "He may never get over this, Isabella. May never be the man he was again. You know that don't you, he may never come back."

"He will," Isabella declared fiercely. "I'll help him come back. We'll get him whatever support he needs, and I don't care how long it takes, but we will bring him back."

"It was him who managed to reach Nick and let him know we were friends." Luke nodded towards the CIA agent who was sitting grim-faced and alone a few seats away.

"And even then, it may only be because his voice was familiar and on some basic level Nick recognised it and knew he could trust him."

"Lucky he insisted on coming." Isabella looked more warmly at the man she had previously dismissed as a misogynistic arse.

"He managed to get Nick to his feet. I picked up the blanket because it was all we had to cover him with, and something fell to the floor – a necklace or something – and Nick pounced on it, scrabbling for it on the floor as if it were the most precious thing in the world to him."

"I think it probably was," Isabella said.

They brought him home to England, to a small, private clinic that Sebastian knew, tucked away in a monied area of London, where he lay in a nice room and was examined. Afterwards, the doctor spoke to Sebastian and Isabella.

"The whip marks on his back, arms, and feet are extensive. We've washed and treated them, but they will leave thin scarring which will never fade. There are rat bites on various parts of his body, and although it looks like they were treated – after a fashion – we have given him antibiotics and a tetanus jab just to be on the safe side."

Isabella nodded, unable to speak, grateful for the steadying arm Sebastian placed about her.

"He is malnourished and dehydrated, so we've got him on fluids and I'm prescribing a high protein diet to help boost his system. He complains the light hurts his eyes, but given the conditions you found him in, that is due to long term light deprivation, so should be only temporary. Physically, he will heal. It's his mental condition that concerns me the most."

"Can I see him?" Isabella asked, her voice husky. The doctor frowned. "Please," she begged. "I must see him."

"All right," the doctor relented. "But only for a few minutes. He's exhausted and needs to rest."

When she entered the gloomy room, Isabella realised the thick curtains had been drawn against the bright October sun, so it was lit only by a small lamp placed next to the bed.

He lay on his side facing away from her.

Isabella paused with her back against the solid wood of the door, a horrible reluctance to go any further gripping her.

Angrily, she shook the feeling away.

This was Nick, her Nick.

They had been through too much together for her to let him down now.

Softly she padded over to the bedside and sank into the chair placed there.

His eyes were closed, his arms tucked tightly to his torso and his hands clasped together as though in prayer. Through the purpling bruising on his fingers, she could see the thin chain of the locket as he gripped it tightly.

His eyelids twitched as if the horrors of his experience still pursued him through his dreams and, as she watched, his eyes snapped open and he stared at her without recognition, his gaze wild.

"Nick," she whispered, and gently placed a hand onto his still clenched fists. "It's me, Isabella. It's all right, you're safe now."

"Isabella?"

"Yes."

"I thought ... thought you were dead?"

"No, I'm alive. They followed the tracker in my phone right to The Preacher's base. They rescued me just in time."

"Good."

His eyes wandered away from hers as if their conversation were done.

"Nick," she whispered. "I'm sorry it took us so long to find you. I promise, we looked everywhere we could but there was no trace of you."

"That's because I was dead," he murmured.

"No, no, you're alive, Nick." Desperately, Isabella placed her hand, warm and strong against his cheek.

"Feel, feel my touch on your face. You're alive and you're with me, and I love you, so very much." Her words choked on a sob.

"Don't cry," Nick murmured. "Please don't cry. Isabella Santorini cries for no one."

"I cry for you," she whispered.

"Don't cry for me," he said. "I'm not worth crying for," and again his gaze slid by her as if he were seeing things in the shadows.

Not understanding why her tears were distressing him, only knowing they were, Isabella took a tissue from the box on the bedstand and wiped her eyes.

"You're safe now, Nick."

"Am I?" He looked at her then and her heart broke at the desolation in his eyes.

"Yes, you are," she told him firmly. "And when the doctor says you're strong enough, you're coming home with me."

She thought she was prepared for the aftermath of what Nick had been through. Believed she could cope with whatever lingering effects there would be. Could deal with the consequences.

She was wrong.

Most of the time it was like living with a ghost. Oh, he would go through the motions – to please her – answering her over bright enquiries as to his wellbeing with one syllable replies.

Then he would lapse into an abyss of silence which Isabella couldn't even begin to breach.

For long days, he would merely exist, his gaze fixed on some distant point and his mind simply not there.

But if the days were an agony of silence and isolation, the nights were a torment of anguish and remembered horrors.

Installing him in her super king bed, Isabella would lie beside him watching his eyelids flicker as nightmares raced through his mind.

He would awaken with a hoarse yell, scrambling from the bed to crouch like an animal in the corner of the room. He was terrified of the dark, so Isabella bought a nightlight and its comforting glow seemed to soothe him a little.

Often, she would awaken to find he had dragged the throw down onto the floor and was curled up on it asleep.

He would only allow her to occasionally touch his hand. Even less occasionally he would let her gently hug him – when she would rest her head against his chest and hear the anxious thud of his heart – before he strained away from her.

She understood, she did, but she ached for things to be the way they had been between them, when intimacy was the connection they both craved.

Sex isn't everything, she told herself crossly. And it was true, it wasn't.

But oh, how her body ached for his touch, longed for him to roll to her in the night and gather her up in his arms.

The two CIA agents visited him before returning to America. Their eyes gentle and understanding, they sat before him, cups of coffee balanced on their knees and tried to make small talk.

Before they left, they spoke with Isabella privately. Nick would not be returning to work, they stated.

They had witnessed this kind of burn out in agents before, they said. Even if they recovered, they had inevitably lost their edge and were no longer fit for duty.

They would set the wheels in motion for a medical discharge.

Then they left, and Isabella knew she would never see them again.

Nick didn't like being indoors and instead would spend long hours in her small garden, despite the chill of the October breeze.

Isabella only insisted he wore his new, thick coat and would sit out with him at the small table on her deck.

There was a robin that visited, and Nick's eyes watched the small bright creature as it hopped about.

Seeing how much it calmed and soothed him, Isabella purchased a bird feeding station, happy when it brought a steady stream of birds to the garden and a kind of peace to Nick.

Often, they would eat in the garden, and Isabella quickly realised that the Italian food they had eaten the summer they first met, was Nick's preference, and after that, it was all she cooked.

One evening, they lingered in the garden long after the sun had set.

Shivering in the chill despite the warmth from the new patio heater, Isabella was about to rise and start clearing away their dinner plates when Nick looked at her, really looked at her.

"Thank you," he said.
"What for?"
"For dinner."
"You're welcome."

"It was delicious."

"It was just meatballs and spaghetti," she answered, pleased beyond belief that he had even noticed what he was putting into his mouth.

"They go together well," he said.

"They do," she agreed.

"Like us," he said, and Isabella's heart jumped into her throat.

"Like us," she agreed quietly.

Softly, silently, as the breeze rippled through the nearby shrubbery and a lone night bird began its evening song, Nick stretched out his arm and took her hand in his.

They sat like that, for the longest of times, until it grew too dark to see and they went indoors.

~Chapter Twenty-Three~
"Please, can I help you save Isobel?"

Luke visited, his comforting bulk crowding into her small porch when Isabella opened the door, surprised to see him.

"Luke," she said. "What are you doing here?"

"I was in the area," he explained. "So, I thought I'd drop by and see how things are?"

"Things are … well, they're just things."

Luke nodded his understanding, then followed her through the house and into the warm and inviting kitchen.

"How's Nick?" he said. "Arianna says she's spoken to you, that things are not so good."

"They're not … great," Isabella admitted.

"Where is he?" Luke asked, beginning to take off his thick jacket.

"You might want to keep that on," Isabella advised. "He's in the garden."

"In this weather?" Luke asked in surprise.

The mild days had finally ended with the approach of Halloween and a raw wind was gusting in from the east.

"He doesn't like being indoors, so…"

Isabella shrugged her helplessness at the situation and Luke sighed, zipping his fleece-lined leather jacket up to his chin and following her out through the back door and into the blustery garden.

"Hey, Nick," he said, as Nick turned to see who had come calling.

"Umm, hey ..." Nick floundered.

"Luke came to see how you were." Isabella filled the awkward pause, realising Nick probably didn't recognise the man he had met only once when he brought him out of hell.

"Luke, yes, of course. You're married to Arianna, Isabella's sister-in-law. She's spoken about you."

"Don't believe a word she says," Luke stated cheerfully and pulled out a chair to sit down.

"Umm, no ..." Nick's voice trailed away, and he stared morosely back out into the garden.

"Is the heater new?" Luke asked, gratefully moving closer to its warmth. "I don't remember seeing it before."

"Yes, I bought it a couple of weeks ago. Well, we're spending a lot of time in the garden now and the weather is getting colder..."

Isabella's voice trailed away at the thought that soon it would be too cold even for the heater to contend with, and then what would they do.

"Coffee?" she asked brightly.

"Please," Luke replied, equally brightly.

They drank their coffee in silence, then Isabella – desperate for anything to fill the conversational void – noticed the buff folder Luke had carried in with him and lain on the table between them.

"What's that?"

"Oh, just a new case. A ten-year-old girl has been snatched by her father, and her mother and stepfather are desperate to get her back."

"Really?" Isabella put her cup down in interest and held out a hand. "May I?"

"Sure." Luke handed the file over. "It's a bit desperate really. The little girl is very sick – she has leukaemia – and needs regular treatment. She went missing from her bedroom two days ago and the mother is convinced it's her ex-husband who's taken her."

"What's the story?" Isabella asked.

Beside her, she was aware of Nick putting down his coffee cup and straightening in vague interest.

"Ex is a total loser, buggered off years ago leaving my client to raise the child alone. He's never paid a penny of child maintenance and never shown any interest in his daughter. The mother re-married several years ago, and her new husband legally adopted the child."

"So, what changed?" Isabella asked. "Why is he suddenly now so interested in the child that he does such a stupid thing?"

"Last year he joined the Family of God and His Followers."

"I've heard of them." Isabella wrinkled her nose in thought. "Aren't they in Wales somewhere?"

"Yes, a freaked out, grade A, whack-job cult who don't believe in Western medicine and think a body should be encouraged to heal itself using prayer and natural remedies only. Anyway, the child's parents are convinced he's taken her to stop all the treatments she is currently having – treatments that are necessary to save her life – I might add."

"I think they might be right," Isabella agreed. "So, why haven't they gone to the police."

"They did, but the police are being slow to act. They paid a visit to the headquarters of this cult and spoke to the leader, but he denied all knowledge of both the child and her father. So, the police have got to get a warrant, and of course, it's all taking time."

"Time, she doesn't have ..." Isabella said.

"There's a picture of her in the file," Luke said, and Isabella was sure she heard something in his voice but flipped through the file until she came across the photo clipped to one of the pages.

Beside her, she heard Nick inhale sharply as she spread the file open, and he saw the picture.

A little girl, sitting in a hospital bed with tubes and drips connected to her frail body. Her bald head was tiny against the backdrop of the hospital paraphernalia but her eyes...

Her eyes were huge and dark. Glowing like coals in her small, pale face as she stared out of the photo at them, she looked like...

Her ... Isabella realised. The child looked like a younger version of herself.

"What's her name?"

Nick spoke for the first time and Isabella glanced at him, aware of Luke staring intently at the other man.

"Isobel," Luke said. "Her name's Isobel."

There was a long silence in the garden broken only by the breeze rippling through the plants and a burst of bird song from the cherry tree, as the robin alighted on a low-hanging branch and chose that moment to serenade them.

"Isobel," Nick whispered, then wiped an unsteady hand across suddenly damp eyes. "Can I help?" he begged. "Please, can I help you save Isobel?"

"Yes," Luke nodded, and his gaze flickered up to meet Isabella's and in that instant, she realised what Luke had done.

Love and appreciation for her burly brother-in-law swelled in her throat and she swallowed hard, forcing the lump down.

"Yes, you can help," he said again. "I hoped you both could."

Time was of the essence Luke said. As Isabella had pointed out, Isobel was running out of time, and they needed to recover her sooner rather than later.

Be ready to leave at dusk tomorrow, he told them, and when Isabella showed him out, she gripped his hand in a fierce gesture of gratitude.

Then she took Nick upstairs to the gym, and they worked together for hours to begin to force mobility back into muscles grown soft from lack of use.

Gradually, as she attacked and he counterattacked, his body began to remember what it could do – what it had been trained over long, hard years to do.

"That's enough," Isabella finally said at midnight. "We need to get some sleep now. We'll do some more in the morning, but now we need to rest."

Nick nodded, pulling off his sweat-soaked tee-shirt and dropping it to the ground as he swigged thirstily at his water and wiped his face, damp with exertion, with a towel.

As he bent to retrieve the shirt, Isabella saw his back crisscrossed with the thin, ribbon-like scabs that were only just beginning to heal over and wanted to cry.

Schooling her face into neutrality, she was busy gulping her water by the time Nick turned back to her.

That night, Nick fell asleep as soon as they got into bed, but Isabella lay awake for a while watching him, thinking his face looked at peace for the first time since his rescue.

For once, the nightmares left him alone and when Isabella awoke early next morning, it was to find Nick still fast asleep in the bed beside her.

They met Luke and Sullivan at the ICRA headquarters that afternoon, and when Sullivan took Nick to where he could change into night op combats, Isabella lingered to speak to Luke.

"Thank you," she murmured.

"For what?"

"For this, for the mission, for Isobel."

"It was a pure coincidence," Luke shrugged. "Arianna told me that Nick was finding it hard to adjust and I wanted to help in some way, but I didn't know how to. Then, when I saw the photo of Isobel yesterday and her parents told me her name, I knew it might, just might, be the trigger that could reach him."

"I think it has already," Isabella agreed. "He seems more his old self, more involved. So, thank you for that at least."

"It's all right. I figured I owed you one."

"Owed me one? What do you mean?"

"Isabella, I know."

"Know what?"

"Know that it was you who shot Roberto the day he kidnapped Arianna. That you were there and managed to kill him before he could put a bullet in her back."

"Is that what you think?"

"Isabella, it's what I know. I figured it out a long time ago. You saved her, and now it's my turn to help save the man you love. It's the very least I can do."

Isabella stared at him in silence, and then Nick and Sullivan were back, and the moment for talking was lost.

It took five hours to travel from London to Snowdonia in Wales where the cult had established their base.

There were six of them: Isabella and Nick. Luke and Sullivan, a young man with an eagle tattoo on his hand who introduced himself as Danny, and a hard-faced woman with piercing blue eyes who nodded when Luke gave her name solely as Smithy.

Sitting in the back of the van, Luke took them through the plans and spread out the maps and surveillance footage of the compound.

"At least, being in the UK, there's less chance of them having guns, but it's always a possibility," he said. "So, stay alert."

They all nodded; their eyes serious as they took in all the information.

"Where do you think they will be keeping Isobel?"

Nick was examining the plans with interest, and Luke frowned at his question.

"They've already had one visit from the local police and although they fobbed them off, their leader must know it's only a matter of time before the police will be back with a warrant. She will probably have been moved to a hiding place within the compound. So, look for cellars, attics, concealed rooms, anywhere one small child could be being hidden."

Isabella thought how terrified Isobel must be. To be taken from her home by a man she barely knew and would have only vague memories of would be scary enough for any normal child.

But Isobel wasn't a normal child.

She was a child who was extremely ill, and at ten years old, was able to understand just how sick she was and be aware there was a strong chance she might die.

Isabella glanced at Nick. His eyes were glinting in the light as he stared and stared at the plans, twisting them to see them better in the gloom.

"There's an awful lot of outbuildings," he stated, tapping the map thoughtfully. "Did this used to be a farm or something?"

"I think so," Luke agreed. "Perhaps you and Isabella could take the outbuildings whilst we check out the compound?"

Nick nodded, his eyes bright with interest and determination.

Meeting Isabella's gaze, he smiled at her, and for a moment it was as though the old Nick – her Nick – was back.

~Chapter Twenty-Four~
"We should wait for back-up,"

Traffic was light, and they reached their destination by ten. Even at that reasonably early hour, the compound was in darkness as the van rolled to a silent stop at the end of the lane.

"According to the information we've managed to gather, they live by the rule of early to bed, early to rise," Luke quietly told them. "So, I expect most of the members will already be in bed. If we're lucky, we may be able to get in, find Isobel, and get out, before most of them even realise we're there."

Silently, they climbed from the van and Isabella looked at the squat dark oblong of the old farmhouse sitting at the end of the lane.

"Stay on comms," Luke ordered. "But communicate only if necessary. Right, you all know what to do, let's go."

Using flashlights, they made their way silently down the lane and split up in front of the house.

Luke and Danny set to work picking the flimsy lock on the front door of the house. Sullivan and Smithy slipped away around the corner of the house to check out the outbuildings clustered around what had once been the old farmyard.

That left her and Nick to investigate the jumble of outbuildings located a small distance from the left of the main house. Their torches casting pinpricks of light on the ground by their feet, Isabella looked at Nick, concerned how he would cope with the dark.

But he seemed fine. Moving silently beside her, he tensed at a sudden sound, then relaxed as he realised it was just the screech of an owl.

Reaching the first of the buildings shown on the plans, Isabella realised it was only an old straw bale storage unit. Without sides, it took mere moments to sweep their torches over the cracked concrete floor to realise there were no hiding spaces there.

They moved swiftly onto the next. Black and menacing, it loomed up out of the darkness and they paused outside the door – listening for any sounds from within.

Total silence, apart from the cry of the owl again as it set off on its nightly murder spree. Nodding at Nick, Isabella waited until he creaked the door open just enough for them to slip inside, then quickly followed him in.

Shining their torches over the interior, they discovered various workbenches littered with woodworking and metalwork tools. A squat potter's wheel sat on one and Isabella realised they'd found the barn where the members of the cult made the essential items they needed for their simple, 'back to nature' lifestyle.

Good luck to them, she thought. If that was how they wished to live, then who was she to criticise. No, people were free to live however they chose, but, when they took young, sick children away from their family – that's when others had to interfere.

There was a buzz in their earpieces.

"Anything?" Luke asked.

"Nothing," Isabella replied.

"We've got nothing either," Sullivan confirmed. "We've checked everywhere and there's nowhere they could hide a mouse, let alone a child."

"Well, come on up to the house and help us look here," Luke told them. "The cult members are awake and up and none too happy at the intrusion."

"On our way," Isabella confirmed, looking at Nick as he began searching the space again with renewed determination.

"Nick, we have to go."

"She must be here somewhere," he muttered.

"Nick, we've looked, she's not here. Perhaps they have got her hidden in the house after all."

For a moment, she thought he was going to ignore her and continue to search. But then he followed her out of the barn without a word.

Walking into the main house, they strolled into a scene of chaos. Alarmed members were scurrying around in various items of nightwear. Luke was toe-to-toe with a slender man with a shock of white hair and piercing blue eyes.

"Where is she?" Luke demanded.

"I have no idea what you are talking about."

"Yes, you do. Don't play games with me. Isobel Martin. She's the daughter of one of your members, Graham Curtis. She's ten-years-old and has leukaemia."

"Well, I am very sorry about that," the man stated. "But I don't see what it has to do with us. I've never heard of this ... Curtis person, and there are certainly no girls here matching the description of the one you are looking for."

"He snatched her from her bedroom and brought her here and you took them in."

"And why would I do that?" the man insisted.

"Because of your cockamamie beliefs that an innocent child should be left to die rather than be given the treatment that will save her life."

"Our cockamamie beliefs, as you call them, are none of your business."

"They are when they put a child's life at risk."

"Who are you?" The man demanded. "Who are you to come into our home in the middle of the night and threaten us? I should call the police."

"You do that," Luke told him. "Maybe they'll have that warrant by now."

"And what about your warrant?" the man asked. "How many laws are you breaking by being here without our permission?"

"We are working for Isobel's parents," Luke told him, and Isabella could hear his anger rising.

The man raised his brows and stared at Luke in silence, and Isabella realised they would get nothing from him.

Desperately, she looked around the ring of scared faces staring back at them.

Where was Isobel?

Where were they keeping her?

Time was running out for the little girl, and they needed to find her soon.

Nick tugged at her hand and Isabella looked at him in mute enquiry. Indicating that she was to follow him, they slipped unseen from the house and stood on the doorstep.

"What is it?" she muttered.

"She's not in the house," he told her. "That man, their leader, he's too cocky, too confident. He's happy for us to take that place apart because he knows we'll never find her, and neither will the police."

"So, you think she's not here then?" Isabella asked, her heart sinking.

"No, she's here all right, just not in the house. Isabella, did you notice that small red circle on the ordnance survey map?"

"Umm, no," she confessed.

"I did, it's the symbol for an old air-raid shelter from the second world war. There used to be a military base close to here – an important one – so maybe the owners of the farm were afraid of an air raid and built themselves a shelter."

"Underground…" Isabella breathed and stared at him with renewed hope. "But where? Where was it?"

"Over beyond the outbuildings we searched, in the field next to them."

"Should we tell Luke?"

"No, that would alert the leader that we might be onto him. And besides, just because an old shelter is still marked on the map it doesn't mean it's still there or even useable if it is."

"True," Isabella nodded in agreement.

"Come on, we'll go and check it out ourselves."

He set off confidently down the path and Isabella followed him, the beam of her torch bobbing as she hurried to catch up. Moments later, the workshop loomed up out of the night and they worked their way around to the back.

Standing on the edge of the large field, Isabella looked around with a sinking heart. Where were they to start looking? How could they possibly find it in all this vast empty space?

"Where do you think it might be?" she asked.

"It won't be too far from the house," Nick stated with confidence. "They wouldn't have much warning of an air raid, if any, so it would need to be close enough to get to in a hurry."

"What exactly are we looking for?"

"I don't know, a hatchway, a manhole cover, anything that looks manmade and could be the entrance to a shelter. Sweep out, we'll cover more ground if we split up."

He moved away, his torch sweeping the ground ahead of him as he began to methodically search, his boots scuffing at loose soil and plant life to see what was underneath.

Isabella moved in the opposite direction. Refusing to be daunted by the magnitude of their task, she copied his search pattern. Long minutes passed before static buzzed in her ear and Luke's voice spoke in concern.

"Isabella? Where are you?"

"Searching one of the fields."

"Why?"

"Nick says there's an old air-raid shelter out here. He has a hunch that's where they might be keeping her."

"Right," he sighed. "I hope so because we've got nothing here. We've searched this dump from top to bottom, with that bastard smirking at us the whole time, and come up with diddly squat."

"I didn't think you'd find her in the house," Isabella confessed, and Luke sighed again.

"Me neither, he was too cocksure of himself. We'll come and help you search."

"Please," she replied. "It's a big area."

"Be there in five," he said.

Whilst they'd been talking, Isabella had continued searching and realised that her feet were following a natural trail in the grass.

Stopping, and shining her torch around the area she saw she was right. A path, faint but there, led away into the darkness.

"Nick," she called in excitement.

Moments later, he was there.

"Got something?" he asked.

"I'm not sure," she replied. "Look," and she played the beam of light over the ground.

Nick knelt and carefully examined the bent and broken undergrowth.

"Definitely a trail," he confirmed. "Question is, where does it lead to?" He looked up at her, his eyes shining with the thrill of the hunt. "Shall we go and see?"

"I thought you'd never ask," Isabella replied, her heart thudding at the renewed purpose ignited in his eyes. This was the Nick she knew.

Keeping their torches low, they followed the trail until it terminated at the dry ditch separating this field from the neighbouring one.

Sliding down into the bottom of the ditch, they shone their torches around. A tangle of bindweed sprawled over the opposite bank of the ditch, and Nick looked at it suspiciously.

"Shine your torch over here," he said, and Isabella complied. "I wonder..." he mused, then grabbed a handful of the weed with his gloved hands and pulled it to one side to reveal a dented and rusty looking hatchway.

"Bingo," Isabella said.

Bracing himself, Nick pulled at the hatchway, and it creaked open to reveal a ladder leading down into the darkness. They looked at it, then looked at each other.

"We should wait for back-up," Isabella said.

"We should," Nick agreed.

They looked at each other again.

"Are we going to?" Isabella asked.

"Nope," Nick replied, and fixed his torch to the shoulder of his combat jacket using the special strap designed for the purpose.

Following suit, Isabella looked apprehensively at the yawning black hole before them, then glanced at Nick. "I'll go first," she said.

"The hell you will," Nick said, then realisation dawned on his face, and he put a hand to her cheek. "Isabella, I've got this."

"Are you sure?" Isabella hated asking, but it was so very dark down there, and after everything that he'd been through, all that he had suffered in the dark, she was suddenly afraid that this was expecting too much of him.

"Yes," he stated firmly. "Very sure."

He left a hand on her face for a second longer and her heart leapt at the look he gave her, before he was turning away and climbing down into the darkness.

~Chapter Twenty-Five~
"Are you Nick and Isabella?"

———————◆•◆———————

The ladder didn't descend for very far, barely four metres, before ending in a narrow corridor, its earthen walls braced with rotten planking.

A closed-door stood at the end of it, and Nick paused to allow Isabella to reach the bottom of the ladder and catch up before he was throwing the door open, and they were in the room.

And then there was the confusion of a child screaming and a man shouting. He charged at them out of the gloom, and Isabella swept her elbow up and coldcocked him under the chin.

Gasping for air, he landed face down on the dirt of the floor and Isabella knelt on his back, wrenching his arm up sharply behind him.

"He's down," she confirmed, as the man yelped in shocked pain.

Nick moved to the child lying on the top of an old, rickety bunk bed staring at them with those big, dark eyes.

"Isobel?" he asked, and the child bobbed her head nervously. A pink hat covered her baldness, and she was clutching a thick sleeping bag up to her chin, but there was no missing the pallor of her skin nor the bruised circles under her eyes.

"Who are you?" she whispered.

"My name is Nick, and that's Isabella. We've come to take you home to your parents."

The girl nodded and tried to smile, but the smile turned upside down and tears gushed down her face.

"I want my mummy," she sobbed and held out her arms to Nick.

Instinctively, he caught her as she slid from the bunk, sleeping bag and all.

"It's okay, princess," he said, as waif-thin arms crept about his neck. "I've got you; we're going to take you home, Isobel. Isobel?"

Gently untangling the child from the sleeping bag, Nick looked at Isabella in concern as Isobel's head lolled against his shoulder.

"Isabella, we need to get her out of here. Something's wrong, she's unconscious."

Alarmed, Isabella unceremoniously yanked the man to his feet, pulled his arms in front of him, and snapped handcuffs around his reluctant wrists.

"Move, you bastard," she growled.

"She's my daughter," he whined. "I can do what I like with her."

"Yeah, yeah, tell that to the police," Isabella snapped.

"Isabella?" Luke's voice squawked in her ear. "We're in the field, where the hell are you?"

"We found the shelter, and we found Isobel, but she's unconscious. We're coming out."

With the man moaning about his rights the whole way, Isabella booted him before her up the ladder and into the waiting arms of the rest of her team.

Nick carried Isobel as gently as he could up the ladder, with Isabella helping him get her out the hatchway.

"We need to get her back to her doctor as quickly as possible," Luke said, after taking one look at the prone figure of the child.

"That's a six-hour drive," Nick snapped, concern sharpening his voice. "She might not make it."

"We could take her to the local hospital," Luke said. "Although ideally, she needs to be with the doctor that's already treating her."

But Isabella was already on her phone.

"Kelly? Sorry to wake you, but we need a helicopter and a medic immediately."

The helicopter reached them a mere twenty minutes after Isabella's phone call, and Nick bent over the child he still held in his arms and ran to the helicopter with her.

As he tried to hand her over to the medic, Isobel stirred and tightened her grip around Nick's neck. Crying out with fear when the medic tried to untangle her, the man shrugged helplessly at Nick.

"Looks like you're coming with her," he said.

"You go as well, Isabella," Luke told her. "I'll phone her parents and tell them to go straight to the hospital."

Isabella scrambled into the helicopter and sat on the seat beside Nick. She helped him to do up the seatbelt around him and Isobel, then her hand rested gently on the top of the child's head and her eyes met his.

"We did it," he said. "We saved Isobel."

"No," she corrected. "Without you, we would never have known where to look. You did it, Nick, you're the one who saved Isobel."

He smiled at her words, and she saw in his eyes that in so doing he had also saved himself.

Nick and Isabella jumped to their feet, as the white-coated doctor exited the room to which Isobel had been taken as soon as the helicopter landed at the hospital.

The doctor smiled at their obvious concern, his gaze sliding over their black ops combats and comms units with a slightly puzzled look.

"How is she?" Isabella asked.

"She's awake and stabilised. I think she's going to be all right, but she's missed several treatments and if she hadn't been brought in when she was, well, it might have been a very different story."

"Can we see her?" Nick asked.

"That depends," the doctor replied.

"On what?"

"Are you Nick and Isabella?"

"Yes."

"Then she's been asking for you."

Entering the room, they found Isobel sitting up in bed looking eagerly at the door. A pretty, dark-haired woman sat one side of the bed holding her daughter's hand. A kindly looking man with tired and anxious eyes sat on the other.

The man rose to his feet at their entry and crossed over to them, one hand outstretched.

"Nick and Isabella?" he asked, and they nodded. "Thank you," he cried and grabbed Nick's hand in a frenzied handshake.

"Thank you for bringing our little girl home to us, you have no idea how grateful we are. When Curtis took her, we…"

His face crumpled and he turned away. Fishing a scrunched-up tissue from his pocket, he blew his nose, his shoulders heaving.

"Nick?"

Isobel's little voice drew Nick over to her bedside.

"Hey, Princess," he said, sitting in the chair vacated by her daddy and gently squeezing her fingers. "How are you feeling now?"

"Better, I'm better." Isobel drew a deep breath and glanced at her mother, who smiled encouragingly at her daughter.

"I wanted to say thank you, to you and Isabella." Briefly her eyes rested on Isabella's face. "For finding me and bringing me home."

"You're welcome, Princess. I'm just happy we found you in time."

"See, he *is* as big and handsome as I told you he was, Mummy," Isobel remarked innocently, and her mother's eyes twinkled at Nick's flustered expression and Isabella's snort of laughter.

"He is indeed," her mother agreed.

Dawn had not long broken when Isabella wearily opened the front door and let them both into the silent house.

Home, they were home.

Dropping to sit on the bottom of the stairs with a groan, Isabella fumbled at the laces of her boots, as Nick collapsed onto the hall chair.

"I need a shower," she said, yanking off first one boot and then the other, and massaging her aching feet.

"Me too," he moaned, then looked at her. "Perhaps I could share yours, you know, to save water."

Startled, she looked up at his words, her pulse spiking at the look in his eyes – a look she hadn't seen since before...

"Of course," she replied primly. "To save water."

The moment stretched between them, and Isabella felt her mouth go dry with lust. Then he was pulling her to her feet and his lips were closing over hers, his hands were on her body, and she somehow didn't think they would make it as far as the shower.

"It felt good, didn't it," Nick murmured into her ear, his teeth gently nibbling on her lobe, his hands cupping her breasts as he curled around her in their big bed.

"Uh huh," Isabella sighed with exhausted bliss. "Bit more than good."

"No, not that," he replied, then flushed at the look she gave him over her shoulder. "Well, yes, obviously *that* was incredible, but I meant finding Isobel like that, rescuing her, bringing her back to her parents. That ... that felt amazing."

"I know." Isabella twisted to kiss him, needing to taste and feel him after so many weeks of believing him lost to her. "It was very satisfying. Do you think her birth father will ever try anything like that again?"

"No, I don't think so. He knows the game is up, and he's a coward; he won't dare risk it again."

"Good," Isabella murmured and squirmed back into his embrace, feeling his arms tighten around her and his breathing hitch as she pressed against a sensitive area.

"You do that again," he murmured hoarsely, "and you may find you have problems walking in the morning."

"Really?" she purred and did it again.

A few days later, Nick came to find her when she was making dinner in the kitchen. His face serious, he accepted the glass of wine she offered, then waved her over to take a seat with him at the table.

"We need to talk," he began, and Isabella took a quick gulp of her wine, alarmed by the tone of his voice and his grave expression.

"What about?" she asked.

"About the future, about me, about what I'm going to do with the rest of my life."

"I sort of hoped that you would be spending it with me," Isabella murmured, and Nick's face broke into a smile.

"Of course, I'm going to be spending it with you," he said. "No, I meant, what am I going to do now I'm no longer with the CIA?"

"Oh, I see." Isabella sipped thoughtfully at her wine. "What do you want to do?"

"Luke has offered me a place at ICRA, and I must confess, it's seriously tempting. Being able to save kids like Isobel, that seems like such a worthwhile thing to do."

"It would be," Isabella agreed, then hesitated. "Sebastian spoke to me before he went back to

Italy. He told me that if I wanted to recruit you into the organisation, that it would be fine by him, and then we could work together."

"Now, that *is* tempting," Nick muttered and took a sip of his wine.

"Or I did wonder," Isabella continued thoughtfully. "If you would maybe start writing again."

"And that's really tempting as well." Nick ran a hand over his face in confusion. "Three options and I like the sound of all of them. I wish there were a way I could have it all and do all three."

"Maybe there is," Isabella said, her quick mind darting over possibilities and options. "Maybe there is a way you can have it all."

~Ten Months Later~
"Maybe, one day."

They had been watching the target for a while now. A young girl, aged eleven, she was clustered with a group of other children in a garden surrounded by a high wall.

"Ready?" asked Nick, glancing at Isabella.

"Ready," she confirmed and cupped her hands to give him a leg up onto the flat top of the high stone wall.

Straddling the wall for stability, he reached down an arm and pulled her up after him.

They had picked their point of entry carefully, at the furthest corner of the large garden, in a small clearing behind a strand of dense trees where a compost bin had pride of place.

Dropping down into the clearing, they waited, listening – had they been heard?

No, the screams of the children carried on uninterrupted, and they exchanged glances of relief.

"Do you have it?" Nick murmured.

Isabella rummaged about in the small pack on her back and drew out the cylindrical shaped object.

Thrusting it securely into the ground, Nick took a cigarette lighter from his pocket and held the small blue flame to the bottom of the device.

They then hurriedly retreated to the furthest corner of the clearing and waited, as the wick burnt through, and the device detonated.

There was a loud whoosh, and the device shot skywards like a rocket into the gathering gloom of a summer's evening, to explode in a loud bang. A glittering fall of shimmering stardust writing out the words – Happy Birthday – in brilliant pink sparkles.

There was a split second of silence, then a loud chorus of oohs and ahhs erupted from the garden.

Grinning at one another, Nick and Isabella linked hands and wandered casually through the trees to emerge into the spacious garden where the birthday party of their niece, Lucia, was in full swing.

Scrambling down off the princess pink bouncy fairy castle, Lucia rushed at them.

"Uncle Nick, Auntie Isabella," she shrieked and launched herself at their legs.

The rest of the children gathered around them, Finley and Connor, the twins of Marcus and Grace, exclaiming in loud voices at the coolness of the rocket and their entry, while little Megan put her arms up to Isabella for a big hug.

The adults were emerging from the house now in various states of shock, which quickly turned into rolled eyes and exchanged grins of relief at the sight of the pair of culprits.

"Honestly," Luke exclaimed, as they sauntered up to the house. "We do have a front door, you know."

Isabella shrugged. "We know."

"Can you come to the office on Monday?" Luke continued, looking at Nick. "There's an interesting new case just come in and..."

"Oh no, you don't," Arianna exclaimed following Luke out onto the patio with a plateful of food in time to hear his last words.

"You promised, Luke. Absolutely no shop talk at Lucia's birthday party."

"I know, sorry," Luke mumbled, then glanced at Nick behind Arianna's back – *Monday* – he mouthed, and Nick grinned in agreement.

Working freelance for ICRA whenever they were swamped with cases and needed extra agents was working well, as was freelancing for the organisation whenever they needed someone with Nick's particular skill set.

It was an arrangement that still left Nick plenty of time for working on his novel which he was almost ready to let Isabella read – almost, he promised – but not quite.

Isabella didn't care if it was never ready for her to read, the mere act of writing proved very cathartic for Nick and helped to further ease the darkness from his soul. For that fact alone she believed it was good for him.

Maybe the life that she and Nick lived was not the type of life most people would choose, but it suited them.

Intensely satisfied with their careers, even though it often meant days, sometimes weeks, would pass by without them managing to touch base with each other once – when they were together the connection was intense and passionately explosive.

Isabella looked happily around the garden, thinking that everyone she liked most in the world was there, the only person missing being Kit who was still on her tour of America.

Runaway ticket sales and sold-out venues had firmly cemented Kit's position as *the* new voice, and Isabella was proud that the young woman had won through after all that happened to her over the past year.

Even Liam was there, back in the country for a brief visit, his usually serious expression lightening at the sight of Nick and moving in to hand him a beer.

A connection had been forged between Nick and the youngest of the Blackwood boys that went beyond explanation, but Isabella believed had its roots in shared hardship.

Although Liam thankfully had never suffered anything like the experience Nick went through, still, in his chosen career as a war photographer, Liam regularly visited hell and was on more than a nodding acquaintance with death.

There were Susannah and James, chatting with their respective mothers, and Marcus's mother who was over from the States on a visit, sitting at their table cuddling her ten-month-old grandson, Alfie, as he slipped into sleep.

Seeing her son's eyelids finally droop, Grace eased in to take the sleeping baby from Celeste, and took him into the house, whispering to Isabella and Marcus as she passed that she was going to put him down for his nap.

Isabella smiled her thanks at Marcus as he passed her a glass of red wine.

"Not tempted at all?" he asked, nodding his head at the sleeping baby.

"No, not really," Isabella said. "Not yet anyway. Maybe, one day."

At the other end of the patio, Nick glanced her way and raised his beer to her, his slow smile warming her to the bones.

"Right now," Isabella continued. "I'm too busy enjoying life just the way it is."

The End...

If you have enjoyed reading

Kiss & Tell

Turn the page for a sneak peek at book five of the Blackwood Family Saga

Pitch & Pace

Where the story continues with Kristina Blackwood

~Chapter One~
"All I want to do is scream"

There is no easy way to give bad news, but kindly Doctor Hughes – who had seen her through various childhood ailments, a broken ankle, and other such minor illnesses – did his best.

Feeling sorry for him, Kit knew she should speak, should end his struggles, but was struck dumb, her soul shrivelling at the death of all her hopes and dreams.

"I'm so sorry, Kit," he said, again. "So very sorry. I know you were hoping for better news, but the truth is…"

His voice trailed away, his face collapsing into regretful lines.

Slowly, Kit nodded.

The truth?

The truth was it was over. Her lifelong dream, her passion, her love, her career, her reason for existing, if she was honest … it was all gone.

She would never sing again.

It started with a simple tickle in the throat, which developed into a cough. Though annoying, it had come and gone, and Kit dosed herself with honey and over the counter medication.

She came home for a brief holiday, during which she sang at the funeral of an old friend and mentor, the writer Annaliese Macleod, and everything had been fine.

Flying back to Vienna a couple of weeks later, Kit felt tired, and out of sorts, and the cough returned with a vengeance.

Go to the doctor, her sister-in-law Isabella told her, and Kit fully intended to, but she was busy and forgot, and then it was the dress rehearsal for a performance of Aida at the Viennese Opera House.

Kit would never forget that moment for as long as she lived. Standing on the stage in her gorgeous costume, she'd opened her mouth, but all that emerged was a strangulated growl.

Clutching her hand to her throat, she tried again. Nothing. Gasping with shock, she sank to her knees as the other cast members gathered around in concern, the music stopped, and the director rushed on stage, his face a mask of concern.

She came back to England, home, to her family, and to visit her doctor, who referred her to the throat specialist at the hospital for a series of tests and examinations that left Kit tearful and fearing the worst.

"Take all the time you need," her director told her. "Get yourself mended. Your understudy can stand in for now. We want you to get better so you can come back."

Well, now she knew; there would be no going back.

Polyps, they told her. Undiagnosed for so long, even after surgery they had left scarring on her larynx.

Will the scarring heal? The hospital couldn't or wouldn't say. Instead, it was left to her old family doctor to break the bad news to her.

She would never sing again.

Oh, she could still talk. Be thankful for that. And who knew, maybe some degree of her previous talent would re-emerge, but she would never be able to sing soprano again.

No more would her voice swoop to the highest level and wring tears from audiences touched by the purity of her voice.

For weeks Kit moved in a fog of indecision. What was to become of her now? Her whole life had been dedicated to her craft, so what was she to do now it was no more?

What use was a singer who could not sing?

Her family rallied around, visiting, and fussing over her. They tried to encourage and cheer her, and Kit loved them for it, but it didn't help. Nothing helped, except when she trained with her sister-in-law, Isabella. Continuing to learn self-defence from the tough and capable older woman, Kit would kick hell out of the punch bag and vent her rage and frustration in trying to take Isabella down.

It helped a little. Growling out her anger, Kit would push herself to her limit and beyond, and Isabella, understanding her motives, let her.

Never offering her useless platitudes, Isabella took whatever Kit threw at her and Kit was grateful. Knowing that Isabella had problems of her own, she understood that maybe their sessions were cathartic for the older woman as well.

The love of Isabella's life, Nick Eastman, was missing, presumed dead. Although all avenues to find him were being explored, and Isabella remained positive she *would* find him, Kit saw the fear behind her eyes and knew Isabella doubted.

And so, the women trained and fought together, and found a ragged kind of relief from their individual losses.

Kit drifted through the days and weeks, uncertain of what direction she wanted her life to take.

At least money wasn't an issue. Always frugal with her wages, Kit had considerable savings plus her portion of the inheritance from her father. Being a member of one of the wealthiest families in Britain has some perks, she thought bleakly.

Aimless, pointless, hopeless, directionless – her life was so much *less* now. Even her gallows humour failed to raise her spirits.

In turn, each family member tried to lift Kit from her depression. Each failed. Oh, Kit would smile, raise a glass, thank them for whatever trip or treat it was they'd imposed on her, and agree they must do it again, but the smile never reached her eyes, and the tears were always a breath away.

Long telephone calls were exchanged between the family, during which the topic of conversation always came around to the problem of Kit.

Finally, it was the turn of Marcus, Kit's oldest half-brother.

Taking her to an exhibition of one of her favourite artists at the Tate, he tucked her arm in his as they wandered about looking at the colourful displays on the walls.

Touched by the gesture and knowing that Picasso was not an artist Marcus appreciated, Kit agreed when he invited her back to his office for coffee.

Sitting in the plush splendour of his penthouse office, Kit smiled as Sally, her brother's gem of a PA, softly entered the room and placed a tray of steaming coffee with a plate of her famous, homemade cookies on the table in front of them.

"Thank you," Kit murmured, and the copper painted lips of the older woman raised in a rare smile.

"You're welcome," she said.

"Hold all my calls for a while, Sally," Marcus said, and his PA nodded.

"Of course. Is there anything else I can get you?"

"No, this is great. Thank you, Sally."

Waiting until the door closed behind the trim figure of his PA, Marcus raised a cup and an eyebrow at Kit.

"I suppose you realise the family are worried sick about you?"

Taken aback by his uncustomary bluntness, Kit bobbed her head in an uncertain acknowledgement of his words.

"I understand, we all understand, that this is a terrible blow to you, but surely…"

"A blow?" Kit raised her eyes to his in angry disbelief. "Is that what you all think? That this is merely a minor setback? Something to simply 'get over'?"

"No, of course not." Realising his faux pas, Marcus put down his cup in dismay.

"Tell me something, Marcus. What is the most important thing in your life?"

"Grace, of course."

"Okay, imagine if one day she was gone. Taken away and you knew you were never going to see her again. How would you feel?"

"Well, that's..."

"How would you feel?"

"Devastated." His expression turning bleak at the thought, her brother looked at her with new understanding.

"Exactly." Kit hammered her point home. "Singing was my Grace, my James, my Arianna, my Nick. The only one of you who has even the vaguest notion of what I'm going through is Isabella – and she still has the hope that Nick is alive to cling to. I don't even have that."

Silence fell over the office as Marcus digested her words. He sighed, then placed a large warm hand over hers.

"I understand," he said, and Kit realised he finally did.

"I get what the family are trying to do," Kit told him, "and I love them for it. But it's not helping. I need time and space to come to terms with this, but I'm never left alone. And it doesn't help that everywhere I go in London, I'm reminded of what I've lost. Even travelling here on the Tube today, there were posters for Covent Garden."

"Maybe a holiday?" Marcus suggested, and Kit shrugged indifferently.

"I did think about that," she admitted, "but the whole thought of flying again, of strangers, of being alone whilst everyone is hellbent on having a good time, when all I want to do is scream to the heavens ... not sure I could bear that."

"Well, what about the cottage?"

"The cottage?" Kit stared at him as the simple brilliance of his suggestion settled into her mind with blinding clarity.

"There's no flying involved, it's remote enough that you won't be bothered by crowds of holidaymakers, it's familiar – after all, how many family holidays did we spend there? And best of all, it's right on the Yorkshire moors, so you can scream to your heart's content, and no one would hear you."

Marcus watched as a genuine smile spread over Kit's face and knew, for once, he'd got it right. "Sally?" He clicked on his intercom.

"Yes?"

"Is anyone using the cottage?"

"No, the last time was Liam a couple of months ago, but it's empty right now."

"Good, can you arrange the rental of a car for Kit. Something sturdy, economical, and not showy. Something that won't mind rough moors and a bit of mud."

"Understood," Sally replied, and Marcus knew from her tone that she not only understood but approved of the plan. "When do you need the car for?"

Marcus looked at Kit, then made a snap decision on her behalf. "Tomorrow."

Pitch & Pace

Amazon
eBook ~ Paperback ~ Kindle Unlimited

~About the Author~

Julia Blake lives in the beautiful historical town of Bury St. Edmunds, deep in the heart of the county of Suffolk in the UK, with her daughter, one crazy cat, and a succession of even crazier lodgers.

Her first novel, The Book of Eve, met with worldwide critical acclaim, and since then, Julia has released many other books which have delighted her growing number of readers with their strong plots and instantly relatable characters. Details of all Julia's novels can be found on the next page.

Julia leads a busy life, juggling working and family commitments with her writing, and has a strong internet presence, loving the close-knit and supportive community of fellow authors she has found on social media and promises there are plenty more books in the pipeline.

Julia says: "I write the kind of books I like to read myself, warm and engaging novels, with strong, three-dimensional characters you can connect with."

~A Note from Julia~

If you have enjoyed this book, why not take a few moments to leave a review on Amazon,

It needn't be much, just a few lines saying you liked the book and why, yet it can make a world of difference.

Reviews are the reader's way of letting the author know they enjoyed their book, and of letting other readers know the book is an enjoyable read and why. It also informs Amazon that this is a book worth promoting, and the more reviews a book receives, the more Amazon will recommend it to other readers.

I would be very grateful and would like to say thank you for reading my book and if you do spare a few minutes of your time to review it, I do see, read, and appreciate every single review left for me.

Best Regards
Julia Blake

~Other Books by the Author~

The Blackwood Family Saga

Fast-paced and heart-warming, this exciting series tells the story of the Blackwood Family and their search for love and happiness

The Perennials Series

Becoming Lili – the beautiful, coming of age saga
Chaining Daisy – its gripping sequel
Rambling Rose – the triumphant conclusion

The Book of Eve

A story of love, betrayal, and bitter secrets that
threaten to rip a young woman's life apart

Black Ice

An exciting steampunk retelling of the
Snow White fairy tale

The Forest ~ a tale of old magic ~

Myth, folklore, and magic combine in this engrossing
tale of a forgotten village and an ancient curse

Erinsmore

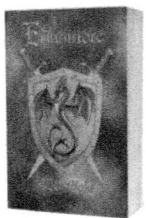

A wonderful tale of an enchanted land of sword and sorcery, myth and magic, dragons, and prophecy

Eclairs for Tea and Other Stories

A fun collection of short stories and quirky poems that reflect the author's multi-genre versatility

Printed in Great Britain
by Amazon